SECRET SWEETHEARTS

A SWEETGUM MEADOWS ROMANCE BOOK 7

IMANI PRICE

First Edition: February 2024

ISBN 978-1-960207-60-9 (ebook)
ISBN 978-1-960207-61-6 (paperback)

Published by Books to Hook Publishing, LLC.
www.BooksToHook.com

CONTENTS

Chapter 1   1
Chapter 2   10
Chapter 3   16
Chapter 4   26
Chapter 5   32
Chapter 6   38
Chapter 7   45
Chapter 8   52
Chapter 9   62
Chapter 10   71
Chapter 11   78
Chapter 12   92
Chapter 13   98
Chapter 14   107
Chapter 15   115
Chapter 16   122
Chapter 17   136
Chapter 18   143
Chapter 19   154
Chapter 20   164
Epilogue   171

Author's Note   177
Also by Imani Price   179

CHAPTER ONE

Focusing on book club was proving to be awfully tough when breakfast smelled so darn good. The aroma of fresh bagels sailed in from the kitchen, and Chrysta inhaled the smell longingly.

She was starving and was way more interested in a bagel than in the book club. Chrysta had heard Rochelle mention the bagels needed fifteen more minutes in the oven. Ever since this announcement, Chrysta had found herself eyeing the time, counting down the fifteen minutes anxiously.

There were two seconds to go.

But Rochelle was nowhere near the oven.

Rochelle had gotten immersed in Mrs. Bridges's account of her favorite part of chapter six. She had quite a lot to say on the subject and not nearly enough to say about the impending bagel situation. Chrysta sighed. The club had started this book last week, and Chrysta was already ahead of everyone else. They'd all agreed to complete three chapters a week, but the assignment was too minimal. So, despite her hectic schedule, she'd gone above and beyond to make it to chapter ten before her fellow book lovers.

And now she was paying for it.

A bagel penance.

"Oh, and when I read that he saw her sneaking in from the bedroom, I almost leaped for joy." Mrs. Bridges trilled, a cup of hot cocoa between her wrinkled hands. She sat a few seats down from Chrysta in the assigned seats that no one had really assigned. They chose the same seats for every meeting. The older women stuck to one side while the younger filled the other.

Since there'd been no space left on the youngsters' side when Chrysta began attending, she gladly sat at the head of the table rather than with the older women. She felt a sense of superiority sitting here by herself. It was like being the CEO at a board meeting or the head of a cabinet. It reminded her of high school when she'd been elected student body president. In fact, many of the faces were even familiar, as the four young ladies at this meeting had attended Sweetgum High along with her. Each one of their faces rang a bell, but she knew nothing about them apart from how they looked and what their names were. Chrysta had broken out her old yearbooks, looking for their faces and names so she could figure out who was who accurately, but she wasn't really friends with them, now or then. When she was in high school, she hadn't socialized much. Friends were a distraction she could not afford, or so she had thought at the time.

If she had known she would be in a book club with them years later, she might have socialized a little more.

One of the young ladies chimed in after Mrs. Bridges finished her soliloquy. "I know! It was the writing for me. I'm not ashamed to say I'd started getting bored, but when I got to that part, I was at the edge of my seat. I said, 'Okay, now we're in business!'" The ever-bubbly Nevaeh chirped between Brandi and Courtney. Whenever she lifted her novel, it would immediately slip from her hands or fall in some way. Nevaeh was constantly falling, tripping, or dropping something.

It made Chrysta nervous. She liked things to be neat, orderly, and contained. Certainly not haphazard, as Nevaeh seemed to be perfectly fine with.

As everyone laughed, the scent of crispy bagels began to irritate Chrysta. At this point, the bagels would be burning. She smiled as the table made more jokes about expecting great twists from the story until the scent grew unbearable. "Rochelle, don't forget your bagels," she blurted, cutting short the laughter. She faced the blinking older woman. "I mean. It's just. It smells like it might be on its way to burning," she muttered.

She didn't understand what the problem was. She only had the bagels and their best interest in mind. Surely no one in the group would want a burned bagel?

"Calm down, Chrysta," said Rochelle. She got up with a bright smile that rivaled the blinding ceiling lights. "I didn't forget my bagels. I just know that these ladies like their pastries well-done." The woman began leaving for the counter while everyone confirmed this. "Don't say anything without me!" She zipped off, and their meeting was forced to pause.

"No one makes bagels quite like Rochelle," said Brandi. She, too, had a mug of something warm. Rochelle never disappointed when it came to refreshments. Since Chrysta began attending these Monday gatherings, the snacks and the drinks had been on point.

It was something she had come to look forward to. Hence why she hadn't eaten prior to this.

Hence why she wanted a bagel.

On the very first night that she'd met snacks on the table, Chrysta had thought they were purchased in a store. The cheese tray had crackers and bread that no average person could just whip up. Rochelle, of course, proved her wrong by happily slapping together something tasty for every meeting after. In the months since Chrysta had started attending, she'd come to learn to anticipate delicious treats every time. It was one of the reasons she didn't regret joining the book club.

One of the few reasons, really.

When she'd first heard who the book club members were, she hadn't been keen on joining. It wasn't that Chrysta despised anyone here but more that she had a feeling they secretly disliked her. During her time at Sweetgum High, she'd chastised people like the younger women at this book club for wasting time gallivanting around campus, *especially* after becoming student body president. She recalled scolding Courtney specifically for attending class late. They'd been in different grades, but Chrysta may have abused her power back then.

She would have apologized for behaving that way, but no one here seemed to recall her authoritative days. Brandi, the subject of a few of Chrysta's tirades, had been who'd approached her about filling the spot of two absent club members. Apparently, the fourth piece to their squad had moved out of town while the other absent club member was traveling the world. In Brandi's appeal, she'd been rather kind and open to letting Chrysta in, and through attending, Chrysta had received warm welcomes. No one had attempted to alienate her despite her history. They acted more grateful than anything. Due to their positive attitudes, she'd shoved her opinions about the other four youngsters aside. High school was a long time ago, and she didn't want to be judged for who she was then, so she was grateful that no one seemed to care. She just wished that they'd stick to the program more when it came to meetings.

"You are *absolutely* right. I can't wait for her to bring them out," Nevaeh added to Brandi's comment. She bent forward to look at the counter. "She should be back soon."

Courtney was rubbing her stomach. "It doesn't matter how much we eat. I can always go for another round of Rochelle's baking." A resounding 'yes' followed her statement. Chrysta's voice wasn't among them, though, and Courtney twisted a little to look at her. "Would you say the same, Chrysta? You look a little dazed."

Chrysta blinked when they all faced her together. Her seat made it impossible to miss each penetrating eye.

Although they were always warm when she settled with them

for meetings, Chrysta *had* noticed that today felt a little off. She couldn't put her finger on what exactly had changed, but something was definitely in the air. And whatever that something was, it was known among her fellow club members but clearly was being kept from her. She may have been looking too deeply into the situation, but her intuition never missed. Upon arriving, some of them wouldn't stop glancing her way. They'd gotten over that habit quickly, but she'd had it on her mind for all of two minutes. It only returned now because of this attention.

"Me? Dazed?" Chrysta asked. She gently slid her empty cup forward. "If it seems that way, then that's not the case. I was just thinking. Caught up in my mind and all that." She smiled, trying to defuse the situation. Her heart, however, pounded a little.

Part of the reason that she hadn't been a big socializer in high school was just like this. Sometimes, Chrysta didn't know what she had done wrong. She just did something, and then others would judge her for it.

The rules were important to her, but when she didn't know them, she felt unsafe. Like she was coloring outside the lines but didn't know what the lines were.

Or what color she was using.

Just then, Rochelle returned wearing red oven mitts to hold a large silver tray of fresh bagels. This sight brought on excited applause, luckily distracting everyone from Chrysta. Chrysta herself clapped, too. She didn't care much for the scrutiny she had been under, and she was glad the bagels had finally arrived. It gave her a chance to share in the joy that everyone else was experiencing. Rochelle beamed, the praise from the baked goods clearly part of the reason she provided such great treats to begin with. "Okay, we can eat and then continue."

Everyone agreed and dug in.

Much to Chrysta's relief.

BOOK CLUB ENDED at nine every Monday, but it wasn't a hard stop. Many of the members stayed later. Usually, when the last views were shared, everyone would linger to chat idly, and people would drift home.

Chrysta normally headed straight home when they called it a night, but this time, she didn't. She'd gotten the strong urge to use the restroom, so she headed to the back where Rochelle said it was.

As she rinsed thick soap clouds off her hands, Chrysta looked at her reflection. Everything seemed in place apart from a strand of hair that had fallen from her bun. She carefully slid it where it belonged once her hands were cleaned thoroughly. It didn't quite fit where it once was, but she left it alone.

She could really fix it up later when she was at home.

She was about to make her exit when muffled voices buzzed through the door. They sounded like Mrs. Zhang and Rochelle. Before, she'd only ever heard their names, but now she knew quite a bit about them. They were the type of women who didn't keep secrets. Neither about themselves nor the people around them, even when the secrets weren't exactly theirs to share. It was safe to say they enjoyed gossip.

Chrysta was going to ignore them like she usually did, gossip not being among her hobbies, when a familiar name caught her ear.

"... Aliyah of all people? I would have never guessed it," said Rochelle in a whisper.

Aliyah. Chrysta's sister.

Who was perpetually in some kind of trouble.

"I was just as shocked as you. They say he's from out of town. What was his name again? Greg something?" Mrs. Zhang's volume was just as low as Rochelle's.

Chrysta wondered if they knew she may be listening. She'd slipped into the bathroom pretty inconspicuously. They'd been caught up in some discussion with Courtney. They couldn't have known she was here. And if they did know, they wouldn't bring gossip on her sister where she could hear it.

She couldn't resist listening closer. She hadn't touched base with Aliyah in a while. For all she knew, her trouble-prone sister could have committed a crime or done something equally scandalous. In fact, a scandal of some kind could be what these two were discussing. Aliyah had been the talk of the town at least three times before. Back in high school, she'd gotten up to enough trouble to make people talk for weeks. In their adult lives, she'd simmered down in terms of mischief but would still have her moments. Chrysta prayed that one of these instances hadn't somehow reached town gossip because once it did, none of Aliyah's secrets would be safe.

Aliyah and Chrysta weren't exactly close, but she wasn't about to sit here and listen to two gossips talk trash about her sister. Chrysta was as much of a rule follower as Aliyah was a rebel, and in her mind, one of the rules was that she wasn't going to stand for people to drag Aliyah's name through the mud.

Not anymore.

Chrysta leaned in. The cold door touched her ear as she listened attentively, ready to figure out what exactly Aliyah had done and why it mattered.

"...Greg is from Sweetgum!" Rochelle sounded irate.

"He can't be. I've never heard of him or his family. You must be thinking of another Greg," Mrs. Zhang sounded the same as she scolded her friend.

"But I've seen him around..."

Chrysta growled at their quarreling. They were saying so much but nothing all at once. Who was Greg, and what did he have to do with her sister? That was all Chrysta was concerned with. What was more worrying was how random town folk knew of this before Chrysta herself. Sure, she and Aliyah weren't close, but she had seen her sister just last week. Surely, if something had been gossip-worthy, Aliyah would have hinted about it. This just proved that whatever connection Aliyah had to this Greg person wasn't any good.

Just as she heard the women's voices fade, a message vibrated on her cell phone, which sat in her pocket.

After opening her messages, Chrysta tilted her head. Her mom just sent a text. "Family dinner?" Their family seldom met since she and her sisters had grown up and moved out. On her own, Chrysta made sure to pay her folks a visit to give updates on her career and plans. She liked receiving congrats from them personally on her achievements. Chrysta couldn't say whether her sisters did the same, but family dinners were an opportunity to share with their parents what they'd been up to. The only thing was that such meetings usually only took place on special occasions.

There was no such occasion on the books. It was just a regular day.

And her mom still wanted to have a family dinner.

Hence Chrysta's confusion. She simply put her phone back and left the bathroom. Did she miss something? Was this sudden family gathering somehow linked to what she'd heard about Aliyah? Chrysta would much rather not deal with an intervention for her sister. She'd gone through too many growing up. She couldn't stand more as an adult.

"Later, everyone." She waved her goodbyes while shoving the glass door open. The warm replies meant nothing as Chrysta stepped onto the sidewalk. August hadn't properly come to a close, but fall was somehow already on its way. Yellow leaves had fallen from the tree outside of Rochelle's apartment.

Chrysta revved her car engine with a head bursting with questions. Calling Aliyah for information may be the fastest way to acquire it. "No," she muttered while spinning her steering wheel. If she called Aliyah now, it would just be putting fuel on the fire. She'd rather not give her sister the attention she wanted. She just knew that whatever mess that girl had gotten into was all in the name of turning heads. That was all Aliyah cared about. It'd been that way since they were kids and was that way now.

She loved her sister. She loved all of her sisters. But she didn't have to like them.

"Whatever." She drove in silence on the darkened streets. They were all grown adults. She couldn't tell Aliyah what to do with herself. If the younger woman insisted on causing mischief wherever she went, then so be it. Chrysta would discover more once they met for this sudden dinner meeting tomorrow night.

A pit of dread formed in her stomach, and she sighed as she drove home. She wasn't looking forward to the dinner.

There weren't even any bagels to look forward to.

CHAPTER TWO

"It's perfect!" A petite young lady in a flowing white gown twirled in the fitting room. Her dress was reminiscent of a princess. Its wide skirt and sparkly fabric gave her dark skin tone an ethereal glow.

The designer held up his chin in clear pride. He took a bow as her parents applauded his creation.

The excited bride-to-be couldn't stay in one place. She began dancing down the short, elevated runway on bare feet. It was positioned at the front of the room. Hanging dresses were draped against the walls on rolling racks, each one a gauzy confection that was guaranteed to make some woman very happy.

The process of choosing the dresses was one that was predictable but still satisfying. And Terrence enjoyed each and every one.

As these theatrics took place, Terrence looked on from the doorway, out of view of the prospective bride, the designer, and her family. It all came together so well. He recalled the long nights he'd spent stitching the troublesome fabric. He'd done the top half while a few colleagues finished the bottom. That specific design had been too tedious for one tailor to handle. Their designer sure had an eye for detail. It amazed Terrance how he always captured clients' desires no matter how vague their descriptions.

"She looks beautiful," Fiona's soft voice floated from over his shoulder, and he turned to greet her. He hadn't seen when she'd followed, but Fiona, who normally worked the front desk, made this comment behind him. It seemed she'd slipped in once the squeals traveled from here to the lobby. Mornings were slow compared to afternoons, so her presence here would not pose an issue.

"I know," said Terrance. His afternoons were normally designated for dress-fitting observation, but this morning, he found himself doing so early. He'd put so much into that dress particularly. It would have been a crime to not witness the grand occasion.

He hurried away from the fitting room once the family packed up. Terrence and Fiona spoke about how well the dress suited the client while going to their stations. Once Fiona sat at the front desk of the glass-windowed lobby, Terrence headed past the wall behind her, where two dresses were on display. A door boasting a body-length mirror was sandwiched between two mannequins. Both wore bright white. They represented what 'Elegantly Made', the custom bridal shop that Terrance worked for, could create for a bride's big day.

Terrance entered a world of sewing tables lining both sides of a small room. Each contained a sewing machine of its own and had a busy sewer at it. There were five tables on each side for the ten people on their staff.

"The dress looks great," he said on his way to his desk of fabrics. He'd been dealing with a particularly tricky dress since the day prior. Terrence sat at the back to keep working, digesting every intrigued hum from his fellow dressmakers. Four were men, and six were women. They had a good mix here at 'Elegantly Made', but some workers were more professional than others. The older folks worked much faster than those who'd only worked here five years at most.

Terrence had been an employee here for over seven years but

still felt like an outsider. His colleagues were sweet and easy to work with, but being from a small town made him self-conscious. Atlanta was the big leagues compared to Peachwood, and 'Elegantly Made' was considered the best shop in the city. Heck, some argued it was the best in all of Georgia. It was insane to think that someone from a town that many hadn't heard of could leave their mark in a dress shop so renowned.

An older woman who sat in front of him paused her stitching to heave a sigh. "Thank goodness!" She clapped her feeble hands, then smiled beneath her red-rimmed glasses. "I was worried they'd hand it to me to make adjustments." She wheezed with a laugh. "I have my hands full with this one right here." Her opened palm indicated the silky white top on her table.

"Wow. So, she couldn't find a single thing that needed improving? It was a perfect fit all round?" A younger guy sat across from Terrance asked with a needle and thread in clutch.

Terrance proudly shook his head. "Nope. I think that this news is enough to motivate us to make today productive. We have a reputation to uphold, so let's work efficiently." He knew that he personally had gotten a boost from watching the display earlier. Hopefully, he'd meet all of his goals for today early.

Someone opened the door and poked their head out just then. It was Fiona again. "Terrance, we need you on measurements. A new client just stepped in, and she's as ready as someone can be to get the process started."

"Oh, okay. Yes. I do remember someone making an appointment. I'm coming." Terrance hopped off his stool and snatched the rolled-up measuring tape beside his sewing machine. He placed it around his neck on his way to the door. It seemed that the more hectic side of business would start early.

He was pleasant with the eager young woman who'd come with her parents. As he'd recorded measurements for years now, Terrance handled the measuring process quickly for the soon-to-be bride. He'd done so in the lobby beside Fiona's desk. While making light conversation with the client, two more future brides sounded the doorbell with their entrance. He'd noticed them in his peripheral vision through the glass. Once he finished up the first, he did the others in record time. By then, the designer had come out to listen to their desires. The man put together a rough sketch on Fiona's desk, then handed it to Terrance to bring to the sewing room.

Terrance had had a handful more measurements to deal with before sliding back into his station. He'd known exactly who to hand the rough sketch to. The older workers tended to cut cloth faster and with more accuracy. As they dealt with that, he sat to tackle the work he'd planned to complete for the day.

Lunch time snuck up on him as Terrance worked with precision to mark and pin dresses together. He handed his work over to the older woman in front of him and then said his goodbyes while leaving to eat.

Upon returning, Terrance sat down to work on alterations. He dedicated a great deal of focus to expanding the bust of a dress that one woman wound up being a size too large for. As he whistled, he tried to imagine how she'd appear once her gown fit perfectly.

She would look amazing.

Terrance was an all-purpose tailor, and he made just as many efforts with menswear as with bridal dresses, but he enjoyed the work with bridal dresses the most. He'd been told to pursue suit-making by a few friends and family in the past but couldn't give up watching the sheer joy of a bride wearing a perfectly fitted dress. Though his days were filled with mountains of work, he appreciated the reward of seeing women's smiles. Every girl deserved to feel gorgeous on her big day. If he could be a part of that, then Terrance had the best job in the world. It helped that 'Elegantly Made' had such a strong reputation. He felt honored to share in its legacy. Anyone from his small town in Peachwood would be grateful for a chance to add to something so profound.

His day flew by, the hours melting into each other until the diminished angle of the light in the shop caused him to look up. "It's late," Terrance checked the time on his cell phone after finishing some adjustments. He surveyed the silent room of diligent sewers. Unlike most of his coworkers, who lived in Atlanta, Terrance had quite a long drive awaiting him. "Guys, I think I'm going to call it a day."

The light reflecting off the older seamstress' glasses was hard to miss when they lifted their heads to sound a unanimous goodbye. "Take care, hon." He assembled his things and strutted off after receiving a chorus of 'Be careful' and 'See you tomorrow.'

"Safe commute." Fiona put down her cell phone when Terrance walked past her. As dark had already fallen, she'd flipped on the lights in the lobby. She seemed to be deep in some online filing as he clutched his backpack while bounding to the door. They'd flipped the 'open' sign to closed since 5 p.m. but tended to work overtime to get a head start on tomorrow.

"Thanks," Terrance said after opening the ringing door. "See you tomorrow." He nodded a final goodbye and left the shop with a skip. Today marked yet another productive day of making dreams come true. Sometimes, he did toy with the idea of taking on more menswear, maybe even making suits on weekends, but he would always drop the concept early. Sewing may have been satisfying, but he needed time for himself, and he was happy to sew dresses. His moments spent watching TV series at his own pace in bed were just as meaningful as stitching fabrics.

A distracting horn sound from a noisy vehicle blared on the street beside the sidewalk. Terrance was not alone in his walk to the subway. Atlanta's sidewalks were packed twenty-four-seven. He was just a small dot in a sea of bodies making their way somewhere after dark. Bright lights shimmered from restaurants, stores, and other establishments in the area. The streetlights were minuscule in comparison to their brightness.

At first, Terrance would stop and admire it all on his way back home, but after working here for so many years, he'd gotten accustomed to it. Now, he held down his head like everyone else.

His thoughts drifted back to the day. That petite bride had been overcome with joy. Terrance often relived the most impactful instances of his day. Today, what stuck with him the most was that. It would be a blessing to see her all dolled-up in what they'd put together. The dress was only one piece of a bride's enchanting look. Sometimes, seeing them took his breath away. If he, a simple tailor, could be this moved by the sight of a bride trying on her wedding dress, he wondered how their grooms felt on their wedding day.

He chuckled at the thought of a man's jaw hanging. Terrence wondered if they had ever shed tears of joy. He'd heard stories but had never seen such a thing in real life. He bet it was wonderful. Terrence dedicated so much to making others look dashing on their big day but never considered his own.

"You're thinking in the wrong order, Terrance," he said to himself. First, he'd need to find someone to love wholeheartedly. It had been too long since he'd put himself on the market. Work took over most of his life. He had no time for dating.

Luckily, Terrance hardly thought along these lines. For the most part, he was content with what he did. But now and then, he did wonder what he may be missing out on.

CHAPTER THREE

Being back home brought on both pleasant and unnerving memories. Chrysta definitely believed that there was 'no place like home.'

She just wasn't sure that it was a good thing.

"Chrysta, you're looking well. Look at you. Did you buy the shampoo I suggested? Your hair looks so full of life!" Her mother air-kissed her face in the dining room passage. As expected, the older woman wore a fine dress that complimented her narrow figure. Her straightened hair was wrapped neatly in a large bun behind her head.

Chrysta held her mother's arms after hugging her. "I *did* take your suggestion, and it's worked wonders!" Work tended to fill every crevice of her mind. Chrysta was lucky she'd remembered her mother's advice. If she hadn't, she may never have heard the end of it.

"I made my famous beef casserole," her dad's voice boomed. Her father emerged from the oven with a tray of something appetizing. The aromatic air floating off its surface made Chrysta's mouth water. It seemed this dish was all that was missing. The rest of the table was packed with great food.

"That looks *amazing,* Dad." Chrysta smiled and took her seat across from the chairs designated for her parents. She'd arrived first to this anxiety-inducing family gathering, just like she always did. She prided herself on doing the same thing every time. Her sisters would turn up soon, but for now, it was just Chrysta and the matching older couple. Baby blue was their chosen color tonight. It shaded her father's polo and the dress hugging her mother's body.

Her parents were so constant. Neat. Clean. Organized and well put together. Chrysta appreciated that about them and tried to emulate it herself.

If only she could get her sister to do the same.

"So…" Her mother sat down with a wide smile. "Did you get the promotion? I mean, you must have, right? You've been on top of your work according to our phone calls." The woman clasped her hands behind her empty plate.

Being the first to arrive was always bittersweet. On the one hand, she was spared the lecture of appearing late, but on the other, she alone would bear her parents' prying. If, for one second, she seemed unsure or revealed bad news, Chrysta could lose their favor.

She always wanted to have their approval.

Chrysta sipped on her glass of water. Her father was at the counter peeling off his oven mitts. "The promotion?" She swallowed harshly as her mother's brows shot up expectantly. "Oh, you know. It's…"

"Look who's here!" Aliyah popped up in the dining room doorway with a stranger on her arm.

Immediately, all attention diverted from Chrysta as her parents welcomed her sister with open arms. They seemed extremely proud of her presence. The two also appeared familiar with who she'd brought.

Chrysta assumed this was Greg, the man she'd heard of through the bathroom door. Why would Aliyah fill their parents in on this new guy in her life and not Chrysta? They weren't the closest, but when it came to drastic developments, they normally updated each other. At least when they caught up every month.

Chrysta swallowed her hurt with a sip of water and forced a smile on her face. Aliyah probably had her reasons.

It was more important now to be welcoming and gracious. The type of sister everyone expected her to be.

Regardless of how she felt.

"It's so good to finally meet you." Greg's voice was deep and full of character. He sounded like a salesman or real estate agent and wore a dashing suit with a low haircut. The scent of expensive cologne wafted off his body. "Hi there. Chrysta, right?" he said after greeting their parents. The man pinned his coat to approach Chrysta.

She smiled tightly as Aliyah ran her mouth before sitting at her side. "Yes. Chrysta." What a debonair man. By simply introducing himself, he'd managed to impress even Chrysta. It was the way he'd talked with such sureness and confidence. His perfect teeth may have had something to do with it, too.

"I had a feeling," Greg stretched out a hand and smiled that glossy smile. "Aliyah's told me so much about you." He'd stepped behind Aliyah's chair to reach Chrysta's. The sister was currently scraping her seat forward to get comfortable at the table.

"I can imagine." Chrysta's smile was genuine as she politely shook hands with Greg. As he settled beside a talkative Aliyah, Chrysta tried her best to catch up on what she'd missed. It seemed a lot had been exchanged between her mischievous sister and parents between now and the last time they'd met.

The conversation seemed easy. Greg was so polished his manners seemed to shine. After telling yet another joke that had her father chortling with laughter, her father shook his head. "That's amazing, but come on. We should say grace. Everyone, settle down now," he rumbled, settling into the proper routine. He held their mother's hand and bowed his head.

Chrysta frowned. "Aren't we going to wait for Danielle?" Their other sister usually attended as well, despite her crazy work schedule.

"She's not coming. Something about a big presentation for work tomorrow," her mom clarified. "Now close your eyes, Chryssie."

"Right. Sorry." Chrysta flinched at the nickname, which she didn't particularly like, but held Aliyah's hand and bowed her head.

When dinner was in full swing, Chrysta lost her appetite. She'd packed her plate with mashed potatoes, mac and cheese, and other delicious food but was struggling to consume them. Her heart had sped up the second her parents began asking questions. So far, they seemed more concerned with Greg and Aliyah, but she knew they hadn't forgotten their prior interrogation. Sooner or later, they'd ask for an update on Chrysta's career. She wasn't sure she had the heart to tell them she hadn't been promoted. Another popular question asked by her folks was whether she'd found someone. Normally, they'd seem relieved that she hadn't gotten involved with renegade men like Aliyah, but today, this view may be different.

Aliyah had done something that Chrysta had yet to achieve. She had produced a fine man to bring home for dinner.

Chrysta, by comparison, had not. She had never even come close to doing this.

And she was worried that her parents were going to tell her all about it as soon as dinner was over.

Aliyah dropped her fork to grab Greg's muscular arm. His muscles flexed, visible even through the fabric of his coat. "Tell them more about your two-story house and the process to acquire it. It's so funny how it happened," Aliyah trilled. She seemed absolutely mesmerized by Greg.

A little too mesmerized, in Chrysta's opinion

Chrysta would roll her eyes, but the man somehow had a hold over their parents, too. She couldn't blame everyone here for being enamored. So far, Greg was perfect in every sense of the word. He owned a lucrative business, two cars, and a large house. Not to mention his good looks and charm. Chrysta could not find a flaw in him. How did Aliyah manage to attract such a hunk? This was the same girl who dated a biker for transportation benefits in high school. People grew and changed all the time, but Aliyah hadn't seemed capable of quite so big of a transformation. Her last partner had been a screw-up, too. Chrysta remembered hearing of the many rackets he'd gotten involved with. She could not recall why her sister wound up dating such a crook.

Now, instead of a crook, she was dating a perfect man. One that had her parents absolutely over the moon with joy.

It seemed a little odd, to be sure.

Greg sipped on his juice. "The story isn't all that interesting. It just so happened that a friend of mine in Peachwood was moving at the same time I'd been searching for a new place and decided to sell his to me. He'd only lived in it for a year, so it was practically freshly built. He designed it himself. You guys should check it out."

"It seems like we have to. Was this friend an architect? How did he design his own house?" Their mom cut her chicken and placed a piece in her mouth, her eyes glued to Greg.

"Yes. He *is* an architect. Would you like me to show you some home designs he's sent me? I have quite a few on my phone." Greg slid it from his pocket to show the eager diners.

Chrysta was the only one who didn't lean over to watch. She forced herself to swallow some meat, then tried to have a look at Greg's phone. Unfortunately, Aliyah's head prevented that. "Are all of your friends career-driven and successful too?" She didn't mean to say this out loud, but it resonated oddly loud in the room.

"Yes, actually," said Aliyah with fluttering lashes. "All of Greg's friends are very accomplished. After all, one is expected to surround themselves with others like them when they've made it." The response sounded like a jab, but Chrysta might have been over-thinking.

Greg put the last of his food in his mouth. "That's true, but I think we should try to stay focused on why Aliyah and I said we should meet." He smiled at Chrysta's bright-eyed sister. "As you all know, we've been dating for a while now."

"Yes." Aliyah stroked her silk-pressed hair that went past her shoulders. "And in the six months we've known each other, we've learned quite a lot."

Chrysta almost choked. Aliyah had been seeing Greg for six months? How long had their parents known about this? Was Chrysta the only one left in the dark? Had Danielle known? She wanted to assume they were lying but could not pinpoint why. It didn't seem like Aliyah to stay committed that long.

She would have to compare notes with Danielle later, and she hoped Danielle didn't rat her out to Aliyah.

"We certainly did." Greg smiled his own eyes for Aliyah and Aliyah alone. "And one of those things is that we love each other and would like to spend the rest of our lives together." He grinned when the two older folks gasped. "Which is why I proposed to Aliyah last night."

"Oh my goodness! Congratulations!" Their mother clapped above her head while their dad commended Greg for doing this. Meanwhile, Aliyah slid a dazzling silver ring onto her finger. It had been hidden in a pocket on her blouse all evening. By the look of it, it had weighed her whole outfit down. Chrysta was surprised that Aliyah had even been able to walk with a rock that large.

It must have killed her not to show it off right away.

Or maybe it was just killing Chrysta to find out about it now.

Chrysta could neither think nor feel. As congratulations replaced their casual conversation, she sat, absolutely stunned. "Congrats," she managed to grit out after five minutes. By then, Greg had started to outline how the wedding would go. She'd heard him mention eloping as soon as possible but still couldn't process what she'd heard. One of the three of them was bound to marry at some point, but Chrysta always pictured herself being first because she was the oldest. She'd been first for everything else and had always gotten ahead of her sisters. What was this feeling? Had she fallen behind?

"We honestly can't wait to spend the rest of our lives together. If we could, I'd say to have the ceremony tomorrow, but that's just impossible." Aliyah fluttered her eyelids at Greg with one hand on his. They touched hands on the table, seeming obsessed with one another. It was as if they'd found paradise in each other's eyes, like a cheesy 80's love song. Aliyah sighed like she was put out by the fact she couldn't get married as quickly as she wanted. "So instead, we'll have to settle for marrying in the next three weeks."

Chrysta could not resist reacting. "*Three* weeks? Have you planned how the wedding will go? How many people besides us and yourselves know about this? What about Danielle? What if she has plans? Having something as huge as a wedding in less than two months after being engaged sounds..." It only dawned on her that she was the only one concerned when she stopped, and silence fit snuggly in the space left by her voice. Her parents' judgmental stares were clear indicators that she needed to dial it back with the questions.

"Oh, Chrys. Don't be such a downer," her mom said after dabbing her lips with a serviette. "When it comes to getting married, I say the sooner the better. It's about time one of our girls had her big day." She clapped once and faced her husband. "What do you say, John?"

Obviously, being the loyal husband he was, their father agreed with a firm nod. "I honestly have to say that I'm with you. The guys over at the country club are always boasting about the milestones hit by their grandkids." He laughed. "After a while, it gets tough to listen to them, knowing none of ours have branched out to extend our family name. I am *all* for this rush wedding. As long as you two love birds are sure of yourselves, count me in."

Chrysta's throat tightened as everyone rejoiced at this insane plan. Not only was she uncomfortable with supporting an event that seemed out of nowhere, but her father's choice of words right now also left a bad taste in her mouth. What did he mean his friends at the country club were boasting about grandkids? Exactly how many people was Chrysta considered 'behind'? Why mention this now and not sooner? The chain of sudden revelations made Chrysta sick. It was like for several years; her parents had hidden growing dissatisfaction that only spilled out now because of Aliyah's achievement. Chrysta had thought she'd made them proud by acquiring the upscale corporate job they'd always wanted her to have. Had they always found it insignificant because she hadn't yet started a family?

Even while clearing the table later, these thoughts plagued Chrysta's mind. Her father and Greg were talking sports teams in the living room while Aliyah channel-surfed on the sofa. Now and then, she shared her opinion in the men's passionate conversation. This was reminiscent of the times Chrysta would offer a helping hand to her mom while Aliyah fooled around on her phone somewhere far away, and Danielle would be too lost in her books to notice. Only now, no one scolded her sister for being lazy.

Chrysta sighed while peeping into the living room at her satisfied younger sister. She now carried some empty plates to the counter. Her mother wore gloves to her elbows at the sink while scrubbing them clean with a brush and sponge.

Bile rose to Chrysta's throat as she brought more soiled plates to her mother. The woman had stopped mid-way through asking about her promotion. Would she reignite this conversation beat, or had all the Aliyah drama diverted her attention? Chrysta still couldn't believe how quickly this was happening. To think, she hadn't even known Aliyah and Greg were dating a few hours ago.

"This is all so exciting," her mom finally said after humming quietly for fifteen excruciating minutes. During that time, Chrysta's mind hadn't stopped racing, but she tuned in now to what her mother was saying. "Aliyah is expanding our family name. Could life get any better?" The mother grinned at Chrysta. "The only thing that could make tonight more perfect is another wedding announcement from you or Danielle." She laughed. "But that would never happen. I can't remember if you've ever dated someone at all." She crinkled her brow. "Quite strange for a very desirable woman." She eyed Chrysta's face like an intricate painting. "I must be mistaken... right? You've dated someone important before, right, sweetie?"

Chrysta's stomach dropped to her toes. "Yes. You *are* mistaken. I've dated a lot in both school and after I graduated. Especially following my graduation from college." She'd had a few short flings here and there, but nothing serious. Her job came before everything. "Don't sell me so short, Mom. I just never had someone who I wanted to bring home. That's all." She leaned against the counter with eyes in the living room.

"Oh, I see. Sorry. It's hard to keep up sometimes. Even though nothing much has been happening..." The last part was muttered. She scrubbed down a glass tray that previously held mac and cheese. "Are you seeing anyone now?" Her mother frowned in anticipation.

Chrysta's palms sweat intensely. She almost lost grip on the counter's edge. "Yes. I just haven't introduced him to the family, but things are getting serious," she said with a forced smile. Her body was cold with sweat.

Why was she lying right now? Surely, her mom and dad were just as proud of her because of her career. Right?

She remembered the sheer joy on both her parents' faces as they looked at Aliyah's ring. The way her father had pointed out that he wished he could brag about his grandkids at the club.

They might be proud of her and Danielle for their careers.

But it clearly wasn't nearly as important to them as getting married.

"Oh really?" Her mother turned off the pipe and faced her with intrigue. "What's his name? Is he from here?"

Chrysta was good at a lot of things, but lying wasn't one of them. She smiled and hoped her mother wouldn't notice. "You'll meet him soon, Mom. And when you do, he'll tell you all about what he does and how we met. He actually has a question for Dad, but that's a whole other story." She shifted her eyes to the living room. "But just know we've been seeing each other for some weeks now." Her throat felt knotted as she struggled to speak. "Things are nice."

"Sounds like it, indeed. Ooh. I'm excited. Two new men to add to the family? Maybe you're better off than I thought, Chryssie. Way to go." The woman went back to cleaning and humming.

Those words left Chrysta with a rock in her throat. How pathetic? Her mom was bound to find out she was lying at some point. Why did Chrysta do that? She wanted to take back her words, but the damage had already been done.

She needed to find someone to bring home. Someone who would blow Greg right out of the water and would assure her parents that she was okay. That there was nothing to worry about. That she was also on the track to success, the same as Aliyah.

She needed to find the perfect man.

And she needed to do it soon.

CHAPTER FOUR

his had to be the smallest time frame they'd ever had to work with.

"And I thought the bride who wanted dresses in a month was asking for too much. *Three* weeks? This is borderline preposterous," The older woman who sat ahead of Terrence in the sewing room was packing her things to leave.

Apart from the sudden rush order they'd gotten this afternoon, today had been average. Terrence stitched dresses and measured about seven brides and bridesmaids on top of the latest order. Due to the short window of time to prepare these new ones, he'd decided to make lots of headway early. That was why he'd chosen to stay back tonight.

"I guess it's one of those excited couples who just can't wait to tie the knot." Terrence threw his measuring tape around his neck. His station was packed with fabric and loose gowns for their latest order. The boss had put him on the job since he worked well under pressure. For the next few weeks, these five dresses were all he would work on. The bride had four bridesmaids she'd requested them to sew for. Out of the dress selections they had hanging in the lobby, she'd chosen three that she liked. It would be Terrence's job to combine what she loved most about each style to create something unique.

An old tailor was already standing at the exit. Everyone else had gone home. It was strange for Terrence to be one of the only workers left. He'd always zoom off before his colleagues due to the length of his commute. After all, he had a long way home, and Atlanta traffic was no joke. "You're the one who took their measurements. Did it seem that way?" The old man leaned in the doorway with thumbs hooked in his suspenders. The older folks here had interesting styles.

Terrence crossed his arms and placed them on the desk. His sewing machine seemed ready for action. "Well..." he recalled the chattering bride, her sister, and sister-in-law-to-be beaming over dresses hanging in the lobby. "The groom wasn't with them, but the bridal party looked as chipper as anyone would be over a wedding." He went over some measurements in the notebook he'd written them. As Terrence looked from the stacked gowns to his book, he wondered if staying later would be wise. It was already six-thirty. The thought of excess work after a long day sent an ache through his neck. He held it, rethinking his decision.

"So, you measured all of them?" the woman asked on her way to the door.

"No, ma'am." He suddenly recalled something said by the bride. "I'm missing one measurement." Part of why he'd stayed back longer was because he hadn't measured the maid of honor. "The bride's oldest sister was busy, so couldn't come down. I heard they're all from out of town. Must have been a hassle for her," he muttered and checked his watch again. "I think they mentioned being from somewhere to the south of here a little ways."

"Are they from where you live then?" asked the old man.

Terrence hadn't asked. "Not sure. I guess the more we work with them, the more I'll find out." He gazed tiredly at the glowing honey light on the wall beside his desk. "Anyway. I think you two should get going. I'll just stay here and wait for that maid of honor they told me about. Hopefully, she'll pop up soon." He might as well get some work done while waiting. Terrence slid one gown toward his machine and said his goodbyes to the older ones.

Once they left, he was the only one apart from the cashier who remained. The shop had already closed, but the maid of honor knew to call before knocking. They'd let her in once she popped up.

It took fifteen more minutes, but she finally arrived. Terrence had been summoned by Fiona when she came in. He stopped drawing clean strokes with chalk on cloth to welcome the client.

"Terrence. It's nice to meet you." He shook her hand near the front desk. The shop felt strange with almost no one inside. He could practically hear the air floating around them.

"Chrysta. I'm so sorry for the long wait. Work was just… you know how it is." The well-dressed woman carried a lovely scent on her crimson red suit. From her brows to her lips were made up quite well, and her neck and wrists boasted sparkling silver jewelry. Pearls seemed to be her favorite. She had black hair that frizzed around her face in a twist-out and a winning smile to complete her appearance. Her smile displayed a glint of embarrassment, but for the most part, it was flawless.

She was stunning. Terrence was around women all the time, and he met a great deal of beautiful ones due to the nature of his job.

This one blew them all out of the water.

"I can imagine. Especially when you're coming from far," Terrence said politely. He ignored the softness of her palm, refusing to be flustered by her insane beauty, and released her hand. "Follow me." Fiona opened the short door beside her desk to allow him and Chrysta a path to the sewing room.

When Terrence led her in, he gestured his arm to the back. "That's my station," he explained. He trailed her as her heels clicked on her way there. "There's the first gown." He walked around his crowded desk to lift it from the mountains of others. He handed it over and directed her to a door in the back. Yes, they had a changing room here too. "Just slip it on."

"Right. Of course." Chrysta frowned at the dress while walking to the mirror that served as the door. She spoke softly as she went toward it and turned the knob easily.

Terrence heard her mumble as she closed it behind her. Was she speaking to herself, or had someone called her? It wasn't impossible that she would contact her sister while in there. Or, well, he was assuming she was the other sister of the bride. That bride sure had been talkative. She'd shared quite a lot about herself with him.

He stuck around as more quiet words came from the now-shut room. Eventually, Terrence decided to give Chrysta some privacy. He'd hate to seem nosy.

Once he stepped to the cashing desk outside, Terrence met Fiona packing her things. "Heading home after a long day on the grind?" he said, flashing her a smile while pushing through the small swinging door. Terrence held his hips once, standing in front of her desk.

Fiona fit some folders into her alligator-skinned handbag. She left it beside the register and then blew out a sigh. "You know that for me, the grind doesn't stop here. Ben can only do so much with the kids when I stay out long." She moved a strand of her curly brown hair to the back of her ear. "I bet once Mommy gets home, they'll forget whatever movie he put on to distract them and come bouncing up to me." She seemed both tired and glad to admit this.

Terrence found her home stories heart-warming. "And Daddy will be bounding up to you right along with them." Fiona's husband was a stay-at-home dad, and while he knew Ben loved it, Fiona felt like she missed out on a lot when she wasn't home. He fixed the measuring tape around his neck while trying to recall some of what Chrysta had been saying. He knew it wasn't his place, but Terrence was quite sure that he hadn't seen a phone by her ear while she spoke. Had he been hearing things?

"Seems you know my house better than most," Fiona put her arms on the table and sat. "I won't leave just yet. You only have one more client to see, and locking up is a lot for one person, so I'll just stick around." She faced the area behind her desk, where the door to the sewing room led. "Is the maid of honor really the bride's older sister?" She dropped her voice to ask.

Terrence rotated his shoulder to deal with a knot that sometimes formed when he worked long hours. "Seems so. She looks like her."

Fiona nodded in slow-motion then perched an elbow on the desk. She leaned in. "She looks like her with a fancier twist. I like her style."

Terrence's shoulders jerked as he laughed inaudibly. "I agree. I imagine she's wearing that for work, but she doesn't strike me as the type of person who is often out of place." He thought back to their brief hand-linkage. Why was it that Terrence could still feel the warmth of her palm? "Her name is Chrysta."

"Yes, I heard when she introduced herself," Fiona said in a faraway voice. "I wonder if she's married too." She was looking at the door once again. Mannequins threatened to shroud its form. At first glance, it could be mistaken for yet another mirror. Dress shops tended to have those in abundance. Theirs was no different. "Has to be right? Pretty women like that don't stay single."

Terrence wouldn't speculate, but Fiona's words rang true. He might have heard his mom say something similar when he was younger. The context was the same. She'd been speaking on marriage, telling Terrence he'd be wise to marry as soon as he left college. According to her, if he waited too long, all the loveliest girls would be taken. She'd used the picking of pretty flowers as an analogy back then.

He could see his mother's tired smile now. She'd been helping his dad with daily stretches when she said this. She never seemed to mind waking early to assist the man with anything. Growing up, Terrence had seen this as a testament to her love for his father. Beauty was important to him, sure. He made beautiful clothes for a living. But the connection between his parents had been plenty beautiful, too.

Hadn't that mattered just as much as having a pretty wife?

Terrence shook his head. He hadn't thought about his parents and their relationship in a long time. Why were these memories resurfacing?

"I'll go check on her now," Terrence said, pushing aside his wandering thoughts. Terrence wouldn't want Chrysta to meet an empty room when she stepped out of the changing area. "I'll be right back, Fiona."

Fiona waved while Terrence jogged through the short doorway.

Chrysta was just a client. Another bridesmaid who needed to have a dress and needed it to be perfect. It didn't matter how beautiful she was. Terrence had a job to do.

And he'd be damned if he didn't do it to the best he could.

CHAPTER FIVE

She'd started by mouthing the words in her head, but after the tailor left her alone to change in the room, Chrysta spoke up to hear herself.

Sometimes, she just needed the time and space to do a little complaining. Somewhere that no one could hear her. Where she could really tell the truth to herself.

She'd feel better, eventually. After she got it all off her chest.

So, as she changed, Chrysta complained.

"And it's a shame that I had to drive all the way here to fit a dress that hardly fits for a wedding that didn't exist just twenty-four hours ago," Chrysta grunted and groaned with hands behind her, twisting so she could get into the garment. She stood on an elevated runway to a central platform. Body-length mirrors were abundant in this space.

The bust area of the aqua-blue dress she was fighting with *refused* to fit over her chest. This was precisely the purpose of fitting sessions like this, but after a frustrating day of work, struggling into a gown was the last thing Chrysta wanted to do.

She'd carried the sour mood of last night into work this morning and wound up having an unproductive day. Chrysta had still tackled everything on her to-do list, but doing that wasn't enough for her. Normally, she'd complete her to-do list *and* cover some tasks designated for the following day. But this time, she'd worked much slower than normal. This only served to worsen her state of mind.

After Aliyah's sudden call about dress-fittings in *Atlanta*, of all places, Chrysta had wanted to rip out her hair. It had come at a bad time, too. She'd just finished an hour-long meeting with the person who'd gotten the promotion she'd wanted for months. Being reminded of her family woes right after such an unpleasant encounter had nearly tipped her off the edge. The far distance had only served as more reason to annoy her. Driving to Atlanta from Sweetgum was doable, sure. But driving after work on a weekday? In the traffic that was world-renowned for being so terrible?

Aliyah had to be messing with her. That was the only explanation.

"Get on me already," Chrysta grumbled as she bent and twisted in all sorts of poses, trying to get the dress to slip over her bust. She bent her upper body forward to provide more room for zipping. The smart thing to do would be to go out there and report the narrow-bust problem, but Chrysta would rather die than leave this room unpresentable. She didn't need that handsome tailor seeing her as the mess she felt like. Did all dress shops in Atlanta hire attractive tailors?

He was cute. She could acknowledge that. But the fact did nothing to make her day any better. In fact, it seemed to make it worse. Much, much worse.

Who wanted to meet a cute guy on a terrible day?

She finally got the zip to go up and hopped off the runway. Chrysta adjusted her hair while admiring the silky fabric. It flowed past her waist like running water in a lake. The design was majestic but uncomfortable around her upper body. And what was with this water-like color? Aliyah hadn't yet shared the wedding's theme, but so far, it seemed to be the sea. "It should be a crime to hire tailors that handsome." Chrysta stroked the front of her chest and pulled the fabric upward. "Grooms may lose their brides if he makes direct eye contact with them." Her joke made her laugh, and she felt slightly less miserable.

Chrysta was heading back to the sewing room when her phone dinged on the narrow wooden table near the door. She'd left her clothes and bags there before getting dressed. "And now I'm getting a text. I wonder who could possibly be texting me while I'm here, trying my best to hold my breath in a way that stops this gown from popping right open." She ran on bare feet to the small table and pulled her phone from her handbag.

Some people designated specific notification bells for others. Chrysta was one such person. The sound that went off was specifically for her relatives. She had one for work and another for acquaintances. This could either be Aliyah or—"Mom?"

Her fingers worked with speed to open the message. Chrysta hoped she hadn't missed another spur-of-the-moment event like the dress-fitting outing earlier. Aliyah had posted photos of herself with Danielle and Greg's sister with 'road trip' as the caption. Chrysta only saw these because Danielle had sent them directly to her. It seemed they'd had fun. She would have asked how they'd all gotten time off from work for such a sudden outing but, quite frankly, didn't care enough. Their jobs weren't as demanding as hers anyway.

She pretended that it didn't make her chest ache to see Danielle included when she hadn't been. It certainly wasn't Danielle's fault.

Even though she wished Danielle had at least stood up for her and told Aliyah to include her in the event, too.

Chrysta read her mom's message with great focus. "Chryssie, will your boo be at our next family dinner?" she said out loud.

She threw her head back and groaned. And just like that, she was reminded of the desperate lie she'd told last night.

She pinched the bridge of her nose against the headache forming there, then held her phone down. "She remembers. *Of course,* she remembers." Chrysta herself had managed to shove that disaster to the back of her mind. She'd been too caught up in her own feelings of inadequacy to recall the *stupid* lie she'd told. "Family dinner, family dinner." Her legs paced on their own, and she roamed the dressing room while trying to figure out what she was going to do. The dress, unfortunately, wasn't all the way on yet. But that didn't stop her.

Chrysta made several arm gestures to encourage the generation of ideas. "So, our next family dinner will probably be soon since there's a wedding happening in three weeks, which gives me something like a week to get someone to act as my boyfriend. Oh boy." She held her forehead, which started to ache. "I could just ask the next random guy I see, but what if he says no?" Atlanta was full of bachelors, just waiting to find someone. The city was huge. If she did some driving, she bet she'd find a volunteer. "Or I may find a nut job who scares the family. This is awful."

Somehow, she'd ended up walking back up the runway. Chrysta paced the mini stage with her head spinning. "I could always just say we broke up." That plan would work if her mother's hopes weren't already through the roof. Chrysta's lie served a purpose: to stop her parents from thinking she was behind Aliyah. Saying they broke up would defeat the point of lying in the first place. She bet her mom had already started boasting about Chrysta's possible future wedding.

"Okay, so I... say he's on a business trip." Chrysta snapped her fingers at the brilliant suggestion. She was more than aware that she'd been the one to provide it, but reacting to her spoken word helped with processing. Speaking out loud, in general, was a great way for Chrysta to work through her problems. She'd done this her whole life, and it always made her burdens less unbearable.

The business trip excuse may cause some brows to raise. One thing her mom undoubtedly had was killer perception. To not hear about a man for months just for him to miraculously be on some business trip when the time arose for them to meet would be a blaring red flag she certainly wouldn't miss. Chrysta refused to be seen as both a letdown and a liar by her parents.

Plus, it didn't solve the problem. Not really. Eventually, she would have to produce a man to bring to the family.

And she was still decidedly man-less.

"How did I get here?" she asked the empty room. It was like she was the protagonist of a heartbreaking movie. "From golden child to family screw-up." Chrysta felt a panic attack coming on, the familiar tightness in her chest a sign that she was close to the edge.

Panic attacks were not unusual for her. Ever since graduating from college, Chrysta had frequently had them. She even had anti-anxiety medication for them, but it was safely locked in her bathroom cabinet at home. Here, nearly an hour and a half away from said medication, she was out of luck.

The only option was to talk herself out of it.

"Okay, breathe. Breathe, Chrysta, breathe," she whispered to herself. She forced her mind to focus on her breath. She heaved, breathing in and out.

"Okay. One thing you can see. One thing you can smell. One thing you can…" her voice trailed off. Usually, the advice from her therapist was pretty sound.

Today, she didn't have the focus. She didn't have a lot of stuff that she could see, anyway. She was in the dressing room of a tailor.

Chrysta exhaled. She had enough time to figure this all out. Her mom would receive a response once Chrysta thought of one. For now, she was here at this dress shop, trying on clothes. If she stayed locked in the changing room too long, Terrence may begin to think she had a problem. She couldn't have that. Even if her world fell apart this instant, Chrysta would maintain a persona of perfection. No one but she could know of her trials.

That would have to work.

Plan decided, Chrysta peeled herself out of the dress. She put her outfit back on, taking care to smooth out any of the lines that might have wrinkled. None had, of course, due to the care she took in hanging up her garments.

Still. She couldn't show up to a professional tailor looking like a mess.

She exhaled while strutting to the door. To think, back in school, she'd found the pressure of keeping up her grades a task. If only she could warn her little self about adult life and its trials. Being the top in her class at school paled in comparison to her current struggles. It'd been so much easier to get good grades than be superior in terms of work, relationships, and her social life. Chrysta swore she would one day drown in all these expectations. It seemed the ones she had for herself were much more debilitating than those of her parents. She *had* to be the perfect daughter. It'd been her role for years, and she refused to give it up. Aliyah's reign would soon end. Chrysta was coming back for her crown.

CHAPTER SIX

When Terrence made it back to the sewing room, he found Chrysta just gliding out of the back door. She looked mildly uncomfortable and had the gown he'd left with her draped over her arm. "Everything okay?" He slowed down next to his desk as she stopped there. From here, she seemed to be wound tightly.

"Not really," Chrysta squeaked when she was closer. "Do you have a dress like this in a larger size? The chest seems to be a bit of a problem." She smiled sheepishly while confessing her plight to Terrence.

Terrence chuckled and took it from her. "Yes, we certainly do, but do you like its design?" He stepped back as she faced him in evident relief. It came as hooded eyes and an easy smile on her face. "If you do, and I get you a larger size that fits a little better, we can start marking off what needs to be adjusted." He slipped behind his desk to look through the options he'd brought with him.

Chrysta hesitated in answering.

"Ah, so you'd prefer a different design." Terrence needn't hear more. "No problem. Your sister picked out some other options." He held up two hangers of different dresses in the same aqua shade of blue. "Do either of these seem more appealing to you?" He could already picture her in the short-sleeved, flared-skirt dress he held in his right hand. "I personally think this here will do wonders for you." He held it forward, smiling gently as he offered her the dress.

Chrysta laughed once. "Thank you." She bent her neck sideways while staring from option to option. "Hmm… actually, you may have a point."

Before he knew it, she'd taken the dress he suggested. Chrysta held it against her body and glided back to the mirror-door. There, she held it against her body and swayed, reminding him of an indecisive queen or princess. He may have seen some in movies doing the same when it came to choosing garments.

"Compliments my eyes… should show off my figure… seems snug," she whispered. She spoke softly to herself while Terrence walked slowly to watch. Her tone of voice reminded him of how she'd spoken on the phone earlier. Soft and distinct. Perhaps this was how she addressed everyone? Including herself?

He paused when she turned around swiftly with the dress against her chest. "Is this the same size as what I have on now?"

"Give me a second." Terrence did a quick check on the tag, then shook his head. "This one is a size bigger. I remember your sister providing two possible sizes for you." He clasped his hands. "So does that mean that you'd like to—"

"I'll try this one on. Just hold on a second." She was already marching into the changing room.

Terrence smiled at how the new gown floated behind her moving body. As the door clicked shut, he immediately heard her mumbling once more. It was the same fast-paced speech he'd heard earlier. Was she on the phone again? Terrence doubted that this was the case.

He still preferred to give her room, so he began to make his exit. After five minutes, he'd return from the waiting area. Terrence would hate to impede on her privacy in case she was dealing with personal matters inside of that room.

"Back again?" Fiona was already locking their windows. They'd flipped the 'Open' sign to 'Closed' hours ago. She walked on clicking heels to meet him by the front desk. "How's the fitting going so far? I heard you two having quite the conversation back there." She pushed her bottom lip toward the sewing room door.

Terrence remained behind the desk. He aimed a thumb over his shoulder with questioning eyes. "You could hear us? It wasn't anything remarkable we discussed. She just chose another design to try on. She's changing right now, but…" He scratched his head. The length of his hair surprised him. It had been a while since he'd visited the barber, but feeling the inches brush under his fingers still caught him off guard. An appointment needed to be scheduled. He liked being well-kept at all times. "She keeps talking."

Fiona strolled up to the desk with folded arms and a frown. "Talking to who? You?"

He wasn't sure how to describe it. "It's like she's mumbling while she changes."

Fiona arched one eyebrow briefly, then laughed. "Oh, you mean like when you want something to fit badly, so you force it to cooperate? I've been there before." She shoved open the short door to the back area and stood behind the cash register. "Don't let it scare you. It's completely healthy for us ladies." She winked.

Terrence would expand more but opted not to. Fiona seemed spent. "You can go now. I can handle the rest of the locking. Your kids need their mom." This would be his first time staying back alone. He knew the lock-up procedures since they were enforced constantly, but that didn't stop his nerves from running rampant. Although, something else may be behind them…

Fiona laughed shortly. "You're too considerate." She lifted her bag beside the cash register. "Try not to let the keys confuse you. They're not so different from normal keys once you twist them. They just require an extra hard push when you do so," she instructed while leaving the short door. The worn-out mother bid

Terrence good night and whistled to the glass exit. "Oh, and Terrence?"

He was about to turn around. "Everything all right?" He spread his arms on the counter.

"I get the feeling this maid of honor is single." Fiona seemed mischievous as she left him with this. The woman waved happily and skipped right out.

Terrence heard the signature door jingle as she locked up behind her. "Single, huh?" Why would Fiona tease him like that? He rolled his eyes in fondness and walked calmly back to the sewing room. Inside, Terrence approached his station and made sure that his pins and record book were in order. As he waited out here for Chrysta to emerge, he heard her soft speech rising in volume.

Terrence finally allowed his intrigue to win and tuned his ears to listen in on her words. Was she struggling to fit in that dress, too? If so, he may need to provide another. From his assessment, that one should have been perfect.

Terrence sat on his stool with an ear out.

"… but if I don't find a date, I'll look like a liar. I could make up some business trip he had to leave for, but that may seem suspicious. Mom isn't an idiot. She'd see right through me, and I'd wind up looking like a fool," Chrysta ranted behind the door. She must have believed it was soundproof. It didn't sound at all like she had any intentions of keeping down the racket. He completely understood why she'd believe that. Changing rooms could feel like other worlds. She most likely needed the time to talk herself through whatever was happening. What better place to do that than a supposedly closed-off room where sound could not travel?

Terrence heard as she went on, becoming transfixed on where this would go. "Finding a date should be easy. I'm smart, beautiful, interesting… all it should take is asking one guy, but who?" She groaned, and he chuckled. "Bringing strangers over never works in the movies. This is probably a disaster waiting to happen." She stopped for a second. "But the only other option is to lie. I mean, there *is* the come clean route, but that's completely out of the question. So what? Do I set up a profile on one of those dating websites? That's so desperate!"

He full-on laughed when she whined out her last sentence. Looking for a date for whatever reason seemed to be stressing her out. Had Fiona miraculously heard Chrysta's complaints? Was that why she told Terrence she was single? He'd heard that mothers had baffling intuition. Fiona must have wanted Terrence to assist. Chrysta *was* a complete stranger he'd only met twenty minutes ago, but she seemed to need assistance. He'd volunteer to help if he thought she would accept it.

Well.

Maybe she would. Maybe Terrance *should* give it a try. After all, she was a beautiful woman who seemed to draw him in. Volunteering to be her date wouldn't be the worst thing in the world. Would it?

He turned the idea over in his mind. Would he like to volunteer to be Chrysta's date for whatever she needed a date for?

Terrance was surprised to realize that he would, in fact, be fine with volunteering for that duty.

His willingness to do so may have had something to do with the nerves he was feeling at the moment. Maybe they weren't nerves. Maybe Terrence was excited to be in her presence. He wasn't just around her but also *alone.* From the second their hands had touched in the lobby, his interest had piqued. He wanted to call it a connection but wasn't sure if it was too soon.

But when it came to attraction, only a single moment was needed for such to develop. He wouldn't mind getting to know her better. Even if it was through helping her with getting a date. Terrence didn't know, but something about someone who spoke audibly to themselves sparked his intrigue.

Just then, Chrysta came out in the flowing blue gown. "Okay, this one is definitely a winner." She stopped before him with open arms. "It hangs where it needs to and fits the right places. The only thing is the neck is just a little wide, but other than that, I'd say it's a winner." She smiled at Terrence.

That smile did something to his stomach that most definitely felt like nerves.

Shaking them off, he tried to be professional. He approached her, looking at the dress through a more critical lens. Terrence made his own assessments with just his eyes. He reached for the sleeves and pinched them before eyeing the rest of her garment. "I see that. A couple more areas need closing, too. Just to get that perfect look." He picked up his pencil to make notes.

After fitting pins in appropriate areas and writing down the adjustments to be made, Terrence dropped his pencil. "Okay. I guess I'll see you for your next fitting when I do what needs to be done," he said while removing the measuring tape that hung from his neck.

"Right. Thank you," Chrysta said briskly, nodding to him, then started toward the back.

"Before you go…" He wasn't entirely sure how to say this. His heart was pounding in his chest, and he couldn't believe that he had even said anything.

Was he really about to ask her if she needed a date?

And was he really about to volunteer?

Chrysta turned around with eyes slightly widened. "Is everything okay? Did you miss an adjustment?" She held up the flowing ends of her gown. "I think that everything you wrote was perfect. Once those are done, it'll be exactly what I need to stand out as a maid of honor." He could sense the words were sour on her tongue.

Terrence shook his head. "No, no. Everything is perfect. I just wanted to tell you that talking aloud is known to help with great decision-making." He leaned on the edge of his desk. "I once read that people with the greatest minds talk to themselves."

Chrysta looked absolutely bewildered. It was only a second later that the realization seemed to hit. "Oh," she said, her eyes wide with embarrassment. "I guess you heard that."

It wasn't his intention to embarrass her, but he supposed this reaction was natural. "The walls in the changing room may seem thick, but sound travels through them quite easily," he said, wearing a nonchalant smile. "Look, if you're in need of a date for whatever reason, I'd be more than happy to offer up my *exceptional* acting skills to be the most convincing doting partner you'd need." He did a short bow.

Terrence may have done all he could to ease her into it, but Chrysta still looked horrified. If she were a few tones lighter, the bridge of her nose would surely go red from embarrassment. He was only assuming that she felt embarrassed. In his eyes, there was nothing to be ashamed of, but again, anyone would behave this way in response to being overheard when they thought no one was listening.

"If you'd let me," Terrence spoke again in hopes of breaking the ice.

Chrysta finally snapped out of it. "Wow, um... wow." She blinked, seeming genuinely overwhelmed. "I... I don't..."

He smiled again. "No pressure. It was just a thought."

His heart crumbled, and he turned to go.

Then, one word had him turning back. "Wait."

CHAPTER SEVEN

This whole time, the handsome tailor with the kind eyes could hear her monologuing? To say she was embarrassed would be a gross understatement. Chrysta could hardly conjure up an answer to what he'd proposed. The things she said while talking aloud weren't for the ears of others. She'd included several personal views that could be seen as immature. And Chrysta *hated* being perceived as anything less than exceptional. Was that how Terrence now saw her? This didn't seem true at all, but she could not be sure. She rethought his suggestion and scratched her head. He had to be teasing. The man had heard her childish thoughts and decided to make a fool of her by proposing something ridiculous.

Chrysta opted to play along and laugh at his prank. "Ha. That's hilarious, but what you heard wasn't what you think." She had no clue where she was taking this.

He seemed lost. "Oh. It wasn't? You *don't* need a date for something important soon?" His sarcasm was gentle, almost teasing. "Sorry. I must have heard wrong."

"Wait, wait, no," Chrysta said quickly. She took a long look at the tall, lanky man who'd been tasked with taking her measurements.

"You overheard everything I said, and somehow, instead of being completely freaked out, you… want to help?" Saying it out loud truly made the absurdity of this obvious. Terrence was either understanding to a fault or a little off his rocker.

Something about him felt like he wasn't off his rocker. She had a feeling that he was, in fact, very understanding.

Chrysta just didn't know what to do with that information.

The gentle man smiled. His lips were lush, and straight teeth were stacked between them. "Yes. But only if you're comfortable. You just seemed kind of frustrated from what I'd been hearing." He crossed his arms while leaning back on his desk. The rolled-up sleeves of his pirate-like top made his firm arms hard to miss. Terrence may have been on the slim side but was by no means skinny.

Chrysta could hardly speak. Here she was, thinking that the odds of finding someone willing to go along with her plan were zero. She'd been ready to face soul-crushing humiliation by begging strangers here in Atlanta to comply. Chrysta had foreseen many glares being shot in her direction for even thinking someone would go along with something so pathetic. She'd been sure that she'd inevitably end up coming clean, but now, here was Terrence offering a hand.

She fought the urge to smile. Doing so would only solidify her desperation for him. So, instead of smiling, Chrysta wore an inquisitive expression. "Are you sure? Won't you feel used? I… I wouldn't want to cause any confusion or to exploit someone. I was just ranting out loud, but deep down, I know that it's wrong to deceive and…" His laughter made her stop. It wasn't scornful, but seemed more… like he was charmed. She stopped with warmth tingling her cheeks.

Terrence made eye contact. He had the warmest dark brown eyes she'd ever seen, and it melted her in her heart. "It's okay. I'm the one offering, so there's no need to over-explain yourself. I get it." He tapped his chin. "How about this?" Terrence uncrossed his arms and held the edge of the table he leaned on. "Tomorrow, when you're done with work, I take you out on a date here in Atlanta. I know you're from out of town like your sister, but if you don't mind—"

"Atlanta is fine." Chrysta wouldn't want anyone from Sweetgum catching wind of what she was up to. They may just assume she'd actually gotten a boyfriend, but just in case this plan went awry, she'd prefer to have as few people as possible know of her and Terrence.

"Okay, great. So, I take you out on a date, we talk, get to know each other, and see if we can come up with a charade that will fully convince your family that we've been seeing each other for months," Terrence proposed. "I just think that if we're doing this, we need to at least know each other well enough to sell it."

Chrysta had no complaints and was still half in shock that he had agreed at all. "Yes. You're absolutely right. A date sounds like a great idea."

It was mostly true. It would have been true, except for the fact that she hadn't been on one in ages. Throughout high school, her studies and responsibilities were all she cared about. College was the same, and even now, as a fully functioning adult, Chrysta still prioritized work over her social life. At this point, she wasn't even sure she knew *how* to date. What would they talk about? What would they eat? The questions and logistics flummoxed her. It had been far too long since she'd seen anyone. Heck, part of her wanted to decline this to catch up on work instead.

Except then, she'd be in the same boat. The same canoe, up the same creek, without a paddle.

And she needed a paddle.

She did spend a lot of time working, after all. Her inner voice wasn't one for letting her slack off. When Chrysta wasn't at work, she'd normally find something productive to do, that being completing what she hadn't done during working hours.

But this was just one date. Going out with a gorgeous tailor wouldn't suddenly throw off her schedule, and she'd need him to come to meet the family anyway. It was better to prepare him ahead of time. Work could wait… She was actually quite behind on work due to emotional problems, but if she *denied* Terrence's offer, these problems would persist. By constructing a plan to keep her mom from casting judgments, Chrysta would be being productive.

There. Problem solved.

"Nice." Terrence smiled and pulled his cell phone from the pocket of his pants. They were tailored, but that didn't surprise her. He must have made the top he wore, too. Unless he'd purchased it from someone else skilled with threads and needles. She already had questions filling her mind, and she was filing them away to ask him on their date.

His hand was big as he placed the phone in front of her face. "Can I have your number?"

Chrysta didn't hesitate to type it into his phone. She let him put his in hers, then stopped to stare at him.

He was handsome.

She wasn't sure what her parents were going to do with the knowledge that he was a tailor and not a real estate mogul like Greg, but she didn't linger on the thought.

Beggars couldn't be choosers and all that.

Terrence smiled. "It's getting late. You should go ahead and slip that gown off. I've already recorded what needs to be altered."

She suddenly remembered why she was here. "Oh yes." Chrysta internally face-palmed. How could she forget? "Thank you for… thank you." She turned around and sped-walked to the mirror-door on the back wall.

Terrence's soft laughter followed her. Like everything else, it wasn't mocking or mean but a harmonious sound that invited her to laugh, too.

To her surprise, Chrysta found herself chuckling as she slipped out of the dress.

A date with Terrence wouldn't be so bad. Her problems, apparently, would all be solved by one handsome tailor.

And all she owed him was one date in exchange.

CHRYSTA'S THOUGHTS were a whirlpool on her drive home. Normally, she was at least a little enamored by the bright lights and bold surroundings of Atlanta, but today, she hardly noticed. Even the skyscrapers on Peachtree Street, lit up against the sky, didn't inspire the same amount of awe in her that they usually did.

She was in awe of something entirely different on this commute.

"I got a date," she muttered to herself. And it had happened so fast, too.

Maybe even too fast.

Suspicion flooded her. What did Terrence want with her? Chrysta realized now, after the glow of the moment was over, that she still did not trust Terrence fully for offering himself as her fake boyfriend. Did Aliyah tell him to listen in on her self-talk? Her sister had always ridiculed her for doing so when they were growing up. Plus, it wasn't impossible for Aliyah to suspect Chrysta of lying when it came to having a boyfriend. Both Aliyah and Danielle knew all about Chrysta's non-existent social life. If their mom had mentioned Chrysta's significant other to Aliyah, it wasn't impossible for her sister to grow skeptical and try to set her up for a trap. Aliyah didn't normally concern herself with Chrysta, but in the name of humiliating her, she might.

It was for this reason that Chrysta feared Terrence to be a spy just waiting to expose her.

"He didn't seem malicious though," Chrysta murmured while sailing down the eight-lane high-way leading out of the city. The streets here were baffling compared to back home. She'd been to Atlanta many times, of course, but they were for specific outings. Things like going to the Coca-Cola factory or the aquarium or catching a Braves game. The thought of coming back here for a date kind of frightened her. It was just so much grander than what she knew, and she felt like she'd be out of her league.

Chrysta didn't like to feel out of control or like she was the one who didn't know what was happening.

Maybe she could cancel…

No. She couldn't. Besides, Terrence didn't seem that bad. Even if he was working with her sister, maybe he would be nice to her. Terrence had given off good vibes when they chatted. Plus, Aliyah was probably too caught up with her sudden wedding to concern herself with being childish. But if Aliyah hadn't put him up to this, then what was Terrence's motivation? Was he just a nice person? He couldn't have actually liked her. Chrysta called herself beautiful during her morning affirmations every day but wasn't one to be approached by men. She'd overheard from colleagues that men found her intimidating. At the time of hearing this, she'd felt extremely proud. Someone as career-driven as she was had no time to fool around with men. For so long, she'd been certain that this attitude was right, but now, with Aliyah getting married and her mom being disappointed in her, she didn't know.

Beyond both her mom and her sister, Chrysta felt something else. Something familiar, that when she touched on it in her mind, smarted like a toothache.

Having a man might be something that wasn't on her agenda.

But it also sounded kind of… nice.

Chrysta swallowed air and held it for ten seconds. She gradually released her breath and listened to her smooth engine. Whether Terrence liked her or not didn't matter. She had a date. This was the best thing to happen to her all week. What made things even better was that they'd be away from town to meet. Chrysta could already imagine what the likes of Mrs. Zhang and Rochelle would say if they'd spotted her with Terrence. The two women would spread rumors quickly and easily dig up information on him. Once it got out that he was from Atlanta and hadn't been seeing her before, it would all be over. Her mom would surely hear the gossip.

"Who knows? Maybe they'd have trouble finding info on Terrence," she said as she changed lanes. He lived pretty far, but Chrysta still would put nothing past Mrs. Zhang and Rochelle. When people wanted details, they'd find means to acquire them. "Anyway, they won't see us, so there's nothing to worry about." As long as no one from Sweetgum saw her in Atlanta, Chrysta could rest easy.

She could pull this off.

If only she could figure out what 'this' meant.

CHAPTER EIGHT

S hould he have gone with somewhere fancier?

Terrence could not name the last time he'd taken someone out. With work stealing his hours and thoughts, relationships just weren't something he could entertain. Yet, somehow, here he was, willingly considering the idea of a fake one.

And, he was heartily embracing the date that he was on in exchange.

"I think she'll appreciate the tasty food and ambiance. It's a great place for a first meet-up. Not too intimidating or too laid back either. You chose wisely," Fiona said with encouragement. She seemed over the moon about Terrence's little link-up with Chrysta this evening. The cashier had no details apart from the fact that he'd be seeing Chrysta tonight. Terrence hadn't filled her in on the whole 'fake boyfriend' aspect of any of this. He felt it best to keep this secret from as many as possible. Chrysta seemed embarrassed enough as it was.

"Thanks," said Terrence. He clutched tightly to his briefcase while heading for the exit. He saw hustling bodies through the glass and hoped that their meeting point would not be victim to crowding. It was but a small bistro beside the dress shop. Terrence and some colleagues had eaten there during lunch quite a few times. He could personally vouch for the food's goodness. He truly hoped that Chrysta would enjoy the time they spent under the stars outside the venue.

"I told her to meet me at six, so I'm sure she'll be turning up soon. I want to make sure that she doesn't end up waiting for me. Later, Fi." Terrence left the dress shop shortly after waving.

He joined the crowds of bodies filling the sidewalk seconds later. With every step Terrence took, he thought about Chrysta. Ever since their short meeting last night, he'd had her in mind. There was just so much to wonder about. For example, why she spoke to herself, why pleasing her parents with a fake boyfriend was so important, and how she managed to look so beautiful even when stressed.

The last part made him smile. While she may have seen him as a guy being nice enough to go along with some ridiculous ruse, he honestly couldn't wait to get to know her better. The man found himself walking with haste down the well-paved path to do so. Tonight, the sidewalk trees were adorned with lanterns that filled Terrence with an indescribable warmth. He looked up at the sky, which twinkled with silver stars. It was like the universe had set the mood for a great first date.

It only took two minutes to get to 'Fab Eats.' He noted the couples and friend groups sitting on the patio outside the small restaurant. He greeted a guy sitting cross-legged in front of a casually-dressed woman and sat at the table next to theirs. It was one minute until showtime. He didn't expect Chrysta to arrive at 6 p.m. on the dot since she worked far away. Terrence had already made up his mind to kill time catching up on text messages.

The hum of many conversations swelled in the atmosphere as Terrence responded to unanswered texts from friends. He scratched the stubble on his jaw while reading them. A few funny videos and reaction pictures made him laugh. The world of messages blocked off the chitter-chatter and cruising vehicles nearby.

"Terrence?"

He held up his face. "Chrysta?" According to his phone, only three minutes had passed since he'd sat down.

Another pristine suit dressed Chrysta's slender body. This one came in dark blue. She offered a smile before moving toward the empty seat at his table. "Hi," she said nervously. Her hair was done low in a bun behind her head. He liked how this style gave her face more room to shine. "I hope you haven't been waiting long. I tried to leave work early to come here."

Terrence got up to pull her chair out. The table was circular and carved from glass, with an umbrella erected from the middle. It cast a shadow over their seat. The honey-colored lights outside the nearby restaurant were enough for them to see each other. "Oh, you didn't have to do that. Did you have a lot to do today?" He watched her take a seat and hang her bag on the chair.

Chrysta heaved a sigh and massaged her knees. "You could say that, but that's the case every day with me." She didn't look too bothered by this. She gathered herself, taking a deep breath before shooting him a small smile. "But it's okay. What's work without trials, right?" She placed her hands on the table as he sat.

Terrence noticed the delicate silver rings on her fingers. The cuffs of her jacket rode up enough that he saw matching elegant bracelets, as well as a watch on her wrists. The details were refined and perfectly reflected her clean-cut style. "You're right. I can't remember the last time I didn't have a busy day at the dress shop," he said. He rubbed the side of his neck while she nodded. Movement caught the corner of his eye. It seemed a waiter was on his way from inside to check on them. Terrence turned his attention to the woman across from him. "I hope you like what's on the menu here. Have you ever eaten out in Atlanta?" He watched as she lifted the laminated menu on the table. He had to say she looked even better in the lighting outside than within the shop. Or maybe her face seemed brighter because she wasn't as worried.

"Once or twice on business trips, but I've never eaten at Fab Eats specifically. Is there anything you'd recommend?" she asked as their waiter stopped beside the table.

Terrence held up a finger to the nervous young guy and then pointed to something on Chrysta's menu. "The tapas here are great, but my personal favorite has to be the tortillas. They're fantastic and are what I order whenever I come." He heard her humming in thought. It was a nice sound, and he wondered if she had a good singing voice. He smiled, adding some more context for her consideration. "But the shrimp can be quite savory, too. They have a fantastic recipe for the dip it comes with."

"Is that so?" Chrysta pinched her lower chin as she read.

"Ask the waiter." Terrence poked a thumb toward the fidgeting youngster holding a notepad between restless hands. "Wouldn't you agree that the dip is amazing?"

The waiter smiled. "Yes. It is. Are you a fan of shrimps, miss?"

Chrysta tapped her finger against an item on the menu. "I'll have the blackened salmon, please." The way that she bounced slightly led Terrence to think she was a fan. It was like she'd been waiting to find out they served that dish here.

He smiled at her tiny display of excitement as their waiter scribbled down her order. "And I'll have the fried snapper." Terrence got more comfortable after they were left alone at their table. He leaned back, evaluating his date's reactions. "Are you a fan?"

"Of what? Seafood?" Chrysta locked her fingers on the table, making her rings click. "You could say that. When it's made well, I'd say it's pretty good. I've tried my hands at a few recipes myself." Chrysta held her head up proudly.

"Oh, so we've got a chef on our hands." Terrence laughed. She was confident, which was super sexy. Her mannerisms now didn't match the anxiety-ridden woman he'd met yesterday. He hoped this meant they were off to a good start. The intention may have been to form a fake relationship, but doing so would be easier if they had some semblance of chemistry.

Chrysta chuckled. "I do cook when I can, but I'm no professional. I just throw something together every now and then." She slipped her phone out. "If you want, I can show you some photos."

"By all means." He gestured for her to continue. Terrence reclined while she swiped through her device. Soon, he was shown an image of a tray holding what looked like a shepherd's pie. It seemed like something pulled up online. The lighting and quality of the food were too perfect. "Did you find this on the internet?"

Chrysta held down her phone with a frown. "What? No. I *made* this. It's in my cooking album on my phone." She laughed before quickly swiping through more pictures. "Look. I'm in some. Do you see me?"

Terrence's mouth popped open when he saw Chrysta holding a bowl of gumbo in what he presumed was her kitchen. "Wait, what? You said you *tried* your hands at a few recipes. That doesn't look like trying." He was completely and utterly amazed. "You're a *cook.* These look great, and the pictures are all in great quality. Do you have a cooking blog or something?" He needed more information and quickly.

Chrysta closed her phone and put it away. Something about the gesture made him sad. It was like she had been illuminated moments before, and now she was dimmed. "You're too kind. I don't have a blog. It's just a hobby." She seemed extremely pleased by his reaction, even if some of her enthusiasm was diminished. "I'm not a professional at cooking like how you are at making dresses." She tilted her head, studying him. "How long have you been doing that anyway?"

He still could not shake what he'd seen. First of all, her cooking looked phenomenal, and second of all, each picture had flattered her appearance. He'd gotten to catch a glimpse of Chrysta in a more casual setting and liked it. Even dressed down, she was beautiful. But he may be a little high on the spark he'd felt yesterday. Terrence needed to calm himself. "I've been tailoring for as long as I can remember." Their food was brought to their table. They both thanked the waiter before he went on. "I've liked designing and stitching clothes since I was a kid. I actually designed a few jackets of mine in high school, but—"

"Really?" Chrysta held down her fork. She'd started eating promptly after the food was brought. "You've *designed* clothes?" This information seemed to intrigue her. "So, you're not only skilled at tailoring but designing too?"

As much as Terrence enjoyed her impressed remarks, he couldn't accept them. "No, no, don't get the wrong idea. I'm not as good at designing as I am at tailoring. Designing is more of a hobby. *Not* like how you say cooking is your hobby, but you're somehow an expert, but an actual hobby that I'm only mildly good at." He just had to tease.

Chrysta rolled her eyes while giggling. "Why do I get the feeling you're selling yourself short?" She stuck her fork into her blackened salmon.

Terrence had just bitten into his fried snapper, drizzled in the delicious curry sauce that the restaurant was known for. "I'll show you some designs when we're done eating." He chewed and swallowed. "What other hobbies do you have?" He noticed a couple lower down the patio rising from their place. As they left, the talking around them lessened. Terrence appreciated this greatly. He'd prefer silence while interacting with Chrysta.

"I recently joined a book club, so reading is one. I used to do ballet in high school but stopped once I graduated, but I did win my fair share of state-wide competitions. Let's see... I used to paint in elementary school. I remember participating in quite a few competitions for those too. I also..."

As Chrysta went on, it became abundantly clear to Terrence that he was dealing with an over-achiever. Whatever she did, she excelled at. It seemed like there was nothing she hadn't done, and done well at that. Terrence simply sat in amazement while listening. He quietly ate, marveling at the achievements of the woman across from him.

"And..." Chrysta stopped with a sheepish smile. "I feel like I've been doing most of the talking. Why are you staring as if I'm some kind of strange specimen?"

He held his tongue. The words 'not specimen; muse' had almost left his mouth. It was a good thing he'd practiced self-restraint. Terrence wasn't sure how she'd react to such a strong term after their second meeting. She was just hard to resist. Why was he so enthralled? He'd already imagined creating a dress specifically for her. "I'm sorry. I just like giving people my undivided attention when they speak to me. Especially when they say things that impress me."

"Oh, stop it." She blushed.

"I don't lie, as a rule. You're pretty darn impressive." Terrence smiled.

Chrysta ate some more of her food. "You asked about my hobbies, so I told you some. Though right now, I'm mostly into reading. I don't have time for many others."

"Yes. I definitely feel you on that one." Terrence suddenly remembered why they'd agreed to meet in the first place. "Congrats on being maid of honor, by the way. And congrats to your sister for finding someone special."

Chrysta laughed. "Thank you, but there wasn't much needed to be done to secure that role. But I will tell Aliyah that you congratulated her." She crossed her legs under the table. Now, Chrysta leaned forward with her elbow on the surface. It seemed she'd eaten enough to be satisfied, and her attention was all on Terrence. "It all came out of nowhere, but it's happening."

Terrence put down his glass of wine after quenching his thirst with a sip. "Is that why she put in a rush order?" He sat back and placed his clasped hands on his lap.

"You hit the nail right on the head." Chrysta seemed weary suddenly. As if the mere thought of preparing for the wedding exhausted her.

Yet another couple rose and left the patio. Terrence stole a glance at his watch. It had been an hour, but he wasn't ready to leave. Things were flowing smoothly. Spending the night here with Chrysta felt very appealing. "I see. Why the rush?"

Chrysta scratched the side of her scalp with the nail of her pinky. She patted the area that itched to ensure it hadn't grown fuzzy. "You'd need to ask her that question. Aliyah and her fiancé just seem extremely eager to get married. There's probably more behind the story, but..."

"I had a feeling that that might have been the case," Terrence said. "When you're in love and want to spend the rest of your life with someone, you tend to do crazy things." He sat forward as Chrysta agreed to his statement. "So, when you relay my congrats to her, will you refer to me as her tailor or your fiancé?"

Chrysta seemed surprised by how smoothly he'd steered them back on track. Her frozen face morphed into a pleasant one before she answered. "Would it be too much to ask you to play the role of my fiancé?" She clenched her teeth and shrugged embarrassedly. "If it is, we can just call you my—"

"Sounds perfect," Terrence cut her off quickly before she could get too into her head. He would not oppose. He'd go along with whatever she required of him. She may not have known it, but he'd become putty in her hands over the past hour. He maintained nonchalance outside, but inside, he pictured himself designing gowns just for Chrysta. She just may be the muse he'd wanted but didn't know he needed. "What's our story? Should we have met on a dating app?"

She nodded. "Yes. That may be more believable considering we live so far apart."

"I'm actually from Peachwood, so saying we met in person may not be so far-fetched." Terrence loved the surprised expression that covered Chrysta's face. "Yes. I'm only an hour away from Sweetgum." He crinkled his brow. "That *is* where you're from, right? I overheard your sister mentioning the name."

"Yes! Yes, we're from Sweetgum. I'm just surprised that you commute here for work every day." Chrysta lifted her fork again.

"But I'd still go with the online dating app scenario since we're both busy people. Plus, no one in either Peachwood or Sweetgum has seen us together, so it's more believable."

Terrence saw her point. "Makes sense. So, we met online, and… how long have we been seeing each other? Six months?"

"Sounds like enough to have gotten engaged. Or I could say that this little date right here is when you proposed. I think it'd make sense, considering I don't normally stay out late in a city two hours away from home." Chrysta laughed to herself. "If I told everyone I'd been meeting you for a special announcement, they'd eat it up." She looked quite pleased as she stretched her lips into a smile.

"I see that happening." Terrence parted his arms. "So, I guess we're officially engaged."

They shared a short laugh before Chrysta picked up her drink.

"What about the fact that Aliyah already met me as her tailor? Won't she wonder why I didn't tell her then?" Terrence scratched his chin in thought. "I'd definitely wonder about that if I were her."

Chrysta seemed to think of a solution. She snapped her fingers. "We can say that we wanted Aliyah to have all the attention while dress-shopping. Announcing our secret relationship then may have stolen some of that." She pressed the mouth of her cup to her lips but put it down to keep speaking. "Does that make sense?"

"Of course." Terrence was getting excited, feeding off her enthusiasm. Sharing a secret with someone he was slowly becoming infatuated with was riveting. "I think that's enough for our story. Met online, dating for six months, engaged tonight, and kept it secret from Aliyah to ensure that she got her chance to shine."

"Look who's been taking notes."

"Hey, I take my roles very seriously." He winked at her and was rewarded with a laugh. Terrence loved how she let loose and laughed a belly-full. He was certainly doing something right. "We're all set? Is there anything else you'd like to know about me? You know, just in case there are questions."

Chrysta looked visibly thoughtful. "You can send me more info over text. It's getting kind of late, and we both have a long way to go to get home." She surveyed the area.

Terrence did the same in surprise. Since when did everyone else leave? He watched the lone waiter sweeping up debris at the foot of a table. "That's true." He checked his watch, which read eight-thirty. How long did this bistro stay open? He hoped he and Chrysta hadn't been holding up the process. Talking and listening to her felt so natural that he'd lost track of everything. "Well, it was certainly nice getting to know you." He got up.

Chrysta rose and peeled her bag off the arm of her chair. "It was my pleasure getting to know *you*. I'm so glad you agreed to go along with this insane idea." She held the strap of her bag. "*Thank* you from the bottom of my heart, Terrence."

His name in her voice sounded perfect. "It's my honor." He stepped aside from the table when she did and planted a soft kiss on her forehead. "Until we meet again."

He found that he was looking forward to that moment. He and Chrysta had cooked up a whirlwind romance that stole both of their imaginations. While he wasn't one to date or really engage in whirl-wind anything, Terrence was excited by their ruse.

And he hoped Chrysta was as well.

CHAPTER NINE

When a delivery man holding flowers had appeared in her office an hour ago, Chrysta had been confused.

Now, driving home with them, she found that she was no less confused.

But she was a little flattered now as well.

She stared into her rear-view mirror at the bouquet of roses in the backseat. They matched the red handbag she'd carried to work today. She wondered how on earth Terrence had known that little fact but had dismissed it as just pure luck and good timing.

Every time she looked at the roses, her heart skipped. She couldn't remember the last time someone had done something just genuinely *nice* for her. She may have been lying about being engaged, but one thing Chrysta had told the truth about was dating in general.

She wasn't just out of practice. She didn't know how to play the game at all.

While meeting new people hadn't been her priority, now and then, guys would take an interest in her. She recalled having three arguably serious relationships. The longest had only lasted four months and had taken place in college but had left an impact.

Chrysta remembered every kind gesture performed and how they impacted her.

Mostly because there hadn't been very many gestures to remember.

Sure, she had gotten some good night texts and gifts for her birthday, but none of her exes had surprised her with roses. Even in the prime of their relationship, surprise flowers with sweet hand-written notes had never been sent. Not only had Terrence made her afternoon with the gesture, but he'd also caught her off guard. How ironic was it that her pretend fiancé managed to be better to her than any of the boyfriends she'd had before? Terrence must have been fixed on selling his role.

Chrysta folded her lips to stop a smile. There wasn't much need to go all-out when no one was looking. What was important was ensuring her family fell for the act. People at work weren't so important. "Although…" She cranked up the radio while thinking aloud. "It wouldn't hurt to spur some discussion about him and me." Terrence may have been miles ahead. Everyone at her work place had seen the grand delivery. Maybe if the locals at Sweetgum already suspected something, it wouldn't seem out of nowhere when she showed up with Terrence at Aliyah's wedding. "But the note was a bit excessive."

Hope you're doing amazing, my love ;)

She remembered everything down to the specialized calligraphy used to spell each word. The picture of the small white card she'd found in the bouquet was etched in her memory. No one but she had witnessed its message. Had Terrence thought specifically of her when sending it? Chrysta didn't want to get ahead of herself, but last night's kiss paired with this amazing gift seemed like clues that something else may be at play.

"He's just trying to get into character." Chrysta listened to the weather forecast on the radio. The sky had been clear all day. With fall on its way, the air was starting to cool down. Cool air and a shining sun made for perfect afternoons like this one. It wasn't too hot to roam about, and neither was it too cold to do so. Chrysta would not mind hopping out of her car to stroll along Mainstreet like the residents doing so now. They must have been searching for a place to have lunch. Having already eaten, Chrysta had no reason to trot the well-paved sidewalks. Normally, she'd be at work finishing reports after having lunch early, but today, other plans had been made for her afternoon.

The truth was that she'd taken the afternoon off to help Aliyah with planning her bridal shower this weekend. Right now, she was en route to her sister's apartment in Sweetgum's housing complex.

Knowing her sister, Aliyah would certainly want the best for her party. They'd likely start this meeting at two and only finish at midnight. Luckily, Chrysta had catered for the long-lasting session by completing all her assigned work tasks for today before leaving. It was simply the smart thing to do.

After taking a bend into Aliyah's neighborhood, she revisited her thoughts of Terrence. Whether he'd sent flowers in the name of building a more convincing story or from the kindness of his heart, she appreciated the gesture. No one had ever done something that grand just for her. The good morning texts from past lovers were pathetic compared to Terrence's sweet note and gorgeous flowers.

She parked in the driveway of Aliyah's apartment complex and climbed out of her vehicle. This afternoon's activity was nothing. Next weekend's event would surely be more hectic to plan than a simple party. Bridal showers were just the *tip* of the iceberg. The actual *wedding* would have everyone scrambling.

Chrysta stood outside Aliyah's door with scrapbooks stacked in her arms. Each one contained ideas for how they'd decorate Aliyah's apartment. Since Aliyah had put her in charge of decorating, Chrysta had done her thing and prepared in advance. Danielle was to handle catering while Aliyah herself thought of activities to engage in at the party.

"Coming!" Promptly after Aliyah shouted, the door was opened. "Chryssie!" said the energetic young woman. She had on sweats but was wearing makeup. Her hair seemed fresh, too. There wasn't a doubt in Chrysta's mind that she'd planned to go out later. Either that or Aliyah would document their session for social media.

"Hey Ally. I brought my ideas for decorating." Chrysta waltzed in beside her bubbly sister. Aliyah had always been energetic growing up, but these days, her excitement levels were through the roof. Chrysta would bounce off the walls if she had her big day right around the corner, too.

For a minute, her mind presented an image of her in one of Terrence's gowns and him in a tux.

She quickly shook it off.

Terrence wasn't her real fiancé. And she would do well to remember that.

Aliyah pulled Chrysta out of her head. "Awesome. Take a seat. Danielle left a while back after showing me some bomb recipes for this weekend. I just can't wait to see everyone," Aliyah cooed. She sat on the plush white coach in the middle of her living room, settling regally in while she surveyed the house.

Before sitting, Chrysta observed the mess on Aliyah's kitchen table. The kitchen was a good ten feet away, but she saw it pretty clearly. It seemed Aliyah had been rummaging through decorations before Chrysta's arrival. Streamers, large sheets of cloth, and balloons were a few items she recognized lying around. The counter wasn't too clean either. There were cookbooks and bowls scattered across it. Chrysta could only imagine the type of meeting her younger sisters had had before now.

"Have a seat, have a seat. And don't be afraid to look at the camera." Aliyah plopped herself onto the couch and reached for something on the center table.

And now, Chrysta was aware of the tripod stands holding varying cameras in the living room. "And you really are documenting this." She laughed to herself and sat beside her sister. They'd all done well for themselves in terms of choosing homes. Aliyah's apartment looked handpicked from a home decor magazine. It had a white theme going on and enough space for running. Chrysta hoped that her sister would live somewhere just as nice with Greg.

Aliyah crossed her legs on the couch while holding a pin-on mic. "Of course I am. Now, put this on. It's all going in my mini-documentary, Ally's Big Day!"

Chrysta could not resist sharing her elation. At first, she'd thought her sister's sudden wedding was evidence of her recklessness, but now, Chrysta found herself warming up to the notion. Aliyah's joy was infectious. Chrysta couldn't deny that. She took a seat and put down her scrapbooks. Ring lights and other recording enhancers circled the living room. Aliyah always went all-out when it came to such things. "Okay, so in here, I created a gold and white..."

They talked for thirty minutes before deciding on which theme to go with. Since Aliyah's wedding would be centered around nostalgia, they opted to go classy for the bridal party. While the wedding would take place in their childhood backyard around the small pond they used to play in, the shower would be here in Aliyah's upscale apartment. Instead of wearing soft blue to match the pond from the past, every guest would wear sharp red. In Aliyah's words, they'd be traveling back in time. Her bridal shower would represent her classy life as a woman, while the wedding would take things back to where her story started.

Chrysta agreed with the theme. "Okay, so we're all set. That took a lot less time than I'd anticipated."

"Yes, it did. Maybe it's because we didn't waste any time butting heads like we used to as kids." Aliyah had a good laugh after nudging Chrysta. "Oh, the good old days. You were always so naggy."

Chrysta's eye twitched a little. Had she nagged either one of her sisters, or had she been tasked with things like getting them from A to B or making sure they didn't ruin the family's reputation? "True, but we have to look at the reason *behind* the nagging," she said pointedly to a giddy Aliyah. However, Aliyah's reaction let her know that her sister had certainly moved on from this topic of conversation.

Clearly, she was fine with keeping Chrysta as her 'nagging' older sister.

Aliyah kept bubbling. "Okay, so I have the bridal shower this weekend as well as our family dinner this Friday—"

"Oh yes, the dinner this Friday." Chrysta bit her bottom lip.

Aliyah stopped counting her fingers. "Wait, did you forget about it?"

Chrysta snatched her phone from the center table. "I couldn't if I tried." That dinner was the exact reason she'd started the whole charade with Terrence. "Speaking of Terrence…"

"Hm? Terrence? Who's that?" Aliyah struck a few poses for the camera on her right. She stopped to stroke her long braids that ran past her shoulders.

A cold sweat broke out across Chrysta's forehead. Now would be as good a time as ever to fill Aliyah in. Or more like to begin planting the seeds for her lie. "Who's Terrence?" If only she'd been born with natural lying skills. "Just… okay, I have to confess something." She shifted her knees so they met Aliyah's when they were face to face. "For a while, I've actually been seeing someone in secret."

Aliyah looked absolutely mind-boggled. "*What?* You? Ms. Workaholic Chrysta?" She gasped in an overdramatic manner. "Wait, Terrence is the name of the person you've been seeing? Why does it sound so familiar?" She lowered her face in contemplation.

"The name probably sounds familiar because he was the tailor you'd met at the dress shop." Chrysta supposed it was customary for him to introduce himself to every client. It surprised Chrysta that scatterbrained Aliyah remembered it. With all the activities and excitement going on in her life, Chrysta would think a tailor's name would be the last thing to stay with Aliyah.

"Oh yes!" Aliyah frowned. "Wait, what? You've been seeing the *tailor* in secret? For how long? You just met him the other day!"

Chrysta gulped but remained calm. They'd already built their story. She didn't need to be intimidated by Aliyah's skepticism. Understandably, her sister was probably just confused. "Well, obviously I *didn't* just meet him if we've been dating in secret. You just didn't know about him because it was a secret." She rolled her eyes as if Aliyah was being ridiculous. "We met online. Like you said, I'm always busy. I didn't have time to go out and meet new guys, so I searched the internet and found Terrence. We've been seeing each other for six months, and it's been pretty nice." She got excited to share the rest with her flabbergasted sister. "In fact, it's been *so* nice that we recently got engaged."

Aliyah's face froze in an expression halfway between stunned and skeptical. Eventually, her features morphed into a somewhat strained smile. "*Wow.* Chrysta, that's amazing!" She threw herself onto Chrysta in a hug.

Chrysta felt a squeeze before Aliyah let go. "I know. He would have revealed himself while fitting your dress, but we didn't want to steal your shine. Plus, we needed to wait for the perfect opportunity before letting everyone know about us. I guess Friday's dinner would be the perfect time. If you don't mind."

"Not at all! I can't believe you landed someone so gorgeous and talented. I heard he's one of the best tailors they've got over there." Aliyah seemed extremely impressed. "Look at you. So, after Greg and I seal the deal, you'll be next in line to walk down the aisle. That's crazy. If I'd known sooner, I would have made this a double wedding. I heard a couple of best friends in town are planning one soon."

"Oh no, no. There's no need for a double wedding. This is your moment, so don't even think about me and Terrence." Chrysta was ready to change the subject. "Anyway—"

"Wait, but why did you keep it secret so long?" Aliyah asked curiously.

Chrysta paused. "Well, you know me. I'm a private person. Plus, with work consuming most of my mind, it wasn't something at the forefront. I mean, when Terrence and I would talk, it felt like only *we* existed, but my time spent away from him was always overridden with work and responsibilities, so it never came up." Most of what she'd spoken was the truth. That date with Terrence last night had felt like a dream. She hadn't even noticed how late it had gotten. If Chrysta recalled correctly, they'd been the last ones to leave the bistro. Did that mean something?

"Wow, that is *so* sweet but also sad. You really need to find a better balance. You can't let that company rule your whole life, Chrysta," Aliyah spoke over her before she could answer. "You're dating a tailor, so that means he can make you *amazing* dresses for free."

Chrysta wasn't at all surprised that her mind had gone there. "Aliyah, it's not about what I can get from him, okay? Now, let's do something about the mess you left in your kitchen." She got up and made a beeline for it. "How can you live like this?"

As if on cue, Aliyah groaned and followed her. "There you go again with the nagging. Look, I..." They began to argue while packing up the mess together.

Doing so reminded Chrysta of old times. She had to say she was satisfied with how that interaction went. Despite Aliyah's questions, Chrysta had managed to convince her that she'd actually been seeing Terrence that long. If Terrence pulled off an act as convincing as hers, then they'd surely fool the whole family. "I was worried for nothing," she said to herself.

The family dinner she'd once dreaded was now something to look forward to. Chrysta could see her parents' prideful faces now. It helped that Terrence was charming and gorgeous. All they had to do was play their cards right to sell this. *And I'll finally be back in Mom and Dad's good books.* She loved her sister, but the feeling that Aliyah got to be first at something over her was just too close to failure.

She was so close to getting that failure and turning it into a success that she could almost taste it.

Something strange in her stomach that felt an awful lot like guilt twisted when she thought of Terrence, though.

Sucking in a breath, she frowned. He had agreed to the plan. She wasn't manipulating him.

Even if it kind of felt like that.

"Let's put them in your closet," Chrysta said brightly, brushing this away. She carried some folded fabrics with her to the hall closet attached to Aliyah's kitchen.

"Right behind you." Aliyah followed reluctantly with full arms as well.

CHAPTER TEN

Sweetgum wasn't a town Terrence visited often, despite it being so close to his home, so being here now was refreshing. It reminded Terrence of Peachwood in many ways. As he'd driven along, he'd seen several structures alive with activity. Just like his home, Sweetgum was a town all about community.

Terrence closed his car door and smoothed his collar before stepping onto the freshly cut lawn of Chrysta's parent's home.

He was ready. Being a fake boyfriend felt… safe. Terrence hadn't been a boyfriend in so long; he was worried that he wouldn't do a good job if it was real.

Having it be fake felt like he could try it out. See if he was any good.

He hoped he was.

Terrence stepped up the short flight of stairs leading to the dark blue door and breathed. They'd gone over their cover countless times over text. He'd even sprinkled in a few details about a first date last night that Chrysta went along with. Everything *had* to work.

It took a few seconds for the door to open after he knocked. This situation may have been unique and stressful, but somehow,

Terrence wasn't scared. He'd been anxious while meeting Chrysta for the first time, but ever since they'd started this trick, Terrence's nerves had vanished. He was honestly just glad to be included in such a beautiful woman's life.

The person standing in the doorway looked familiar. "Wow, he really is the tailor from Atlanta. Welcome. We've met, but apparently, you already knew who I was." She smiled playfully and made way for Terrence to enter.

Her face was definitely familiar, and he placed it quickly. Yes, this was Chrysta's middle sister, not the bride but the other bridesmaid. He'd measured her along with the other bridesmaids earlier this week. "Yes, I am. It's great to see you again, Danielle." He walked into the tiled house and was mystified by the scent of fresh food. A level of warmth hugged him as the sounds of laughter floated from the kitchen. "Seems like I came just in time to party." After walking down a short hall, Terrence turned left and entered what served as their dining room. "Hello to everyone."

Danielle slid to his side and held his shoulders. "Chrysta, your fiancé is here!" She seemed glad to share this.

Terrence guessed that Chrysta had already shared the happy news. Good for her.

Now, it was his time to shine.

Chrysta stopped washing dishes at the sink to smile at Terrence. "Terrence!" She washed the suds off her hands and dried them with a towel hanging off one of the cupboards.

When Chrysta bombarded him with a tight hug, Terrence's confidence increased. His heart beat faster as he embraced her and pulled her close.

If being a boyfriend meant this, then he could definitely get used to it.

He took in her perfume and kissed her cheek. He wanted to hold onto her longer but felt her pull back, and he let her. He smiled at her. "Someone's happy to see me. What? Did you think I'd be a no-show at one of the biggest nights of our relationship?" He rubbed her back when she let go, then waved at the rest of the family. "Hey, folks. It's good to finally meet everyone."

"Terrence! The man we've recently heard *so* much about." An older man with his head clean-shaven walked away from the counter. He'd been leaning there with whom Terrence assumed was the groom-to-be and Aliyah. "If you hadn't shown up tonight, I'd be convinced you weren't real." He stretched out a hand to be shaken.

Terrence wasn't sure what to make of this statement. "Well, sir, I can assure you that I am indeed *very* real and so happy to finally meet Chrysta's amazing family." He shook the man's hand and got squeezed. The father had *quite* a grip.

"Yes, you *are* very real and also so handsome!" Chrysta's mom had been refilling the napkin holder on the table. She left that to greet Terrence face to face. "It's so nice to meet Chrysta's secret lover after such a long relationship." She was smiling but also looked doubtful. "Tell me your secret because I don't think I'd be able to fall in love with someone and hide it for as long as you two."

Chrysta laughed in clear discomfort. "Mom, we had our reasons." She'd been standing with her arms around his waist the whole time.

Terrence kept his arm around her shoulders. "We sure did, and I must say that I'm glad we chose that route because now I get to see all of your surprised reactions." Everyone laughed at his joke. "No. I'm serious. This is entertaining." He saluted Aliyah and her fiancé by the counter, then glanced at the table full of delicious food. "This all looks *amazing*."

"Because it is." Danielle sat in her spot and got comfortable. "Come on, everyone. Enough wasting time. Let's eat!"

Chrysta had guided him to sit at her side. They were now at the very end of the table. Luckily, it was large enough that they both fit perfectly. Chrysta's parents had quite an impressive abode. The house Terrence grew up in paled in comparison to this spacious sanctuary with top-notch furniture and state-of-the-art kitchen equipment.

"It feels refreshing having another guy at the table. Soon, we may outnumber the girls." Greg smiled at Terrence as another bout of laughter started up. They'd already said their grace and were digging into the amazing meal prepared by Chrysta's mom. "Terrence, tell us more about yourself. Why tailoring?"

It seemed Greg had become part of the family. He was already interrogating Terrence like he'd been here for ages. Terrence smiled at the other man, willing to meet his challenge. "It's just something I've always loved. Fashion and sewing are my passions. Although I must say that after meeting Chrysta, she's become one of those as well." He winked at the bashful woman to his left.

"Oh, seems we've got quite the charmer on our hands," said Chrysta's father. He laughed while cutting the steak on his plate. "You must be good at what you do since you work at the best dress shop in Atlanta. That's a big city."

"Yes. It's very impressive that you managed to secure a place there despite being from somewhere as small as Peachwood. I feel proud on their behalf." Chrysta's mom looked entranced by him. "Your parents must be proud, too. Having a son that talented must blow their minds."

Terrence smiled. "I'm sure they are." If he got into the details about his folks, he may down the mood. "Sewing isn't that difficult when you have a gorgeous muse."

Chrysta seemed stunned by all the compliments. "You're just bursting with these tonight, aren't you?" She giggled as her sisters chorused in a long-winded 'Ooh.' "Don't listen to him. He got to where he is because of his own talent. I only came into the picture later when we met online."

Danielle put down her fork. "I've never been a fan of dating websites, but you two make them seem like they work. What was the first date like? Were you nervous about meeting in person? I know I'd be." Her eye shape resembled Chrysta's and Aliyah's. Sitting here gave Terrence some insight as to where they got this feature. Their fathers were the same.

They really did seem like a nice family. Terrence would love to marry into a family just like this one.

"I don't know. Somehow, with Terrence, I just had a feeling things would work," Chrysta answered. "And the day we met for the first time in Atlanta proved that. We clicked immediately, and he was just *so* sweet and so kind. I just had a feeling we'd be together a *long* time." She stared lovingly at Terrence, and his heart nearly shot from his body.

He nodded. "I felt the exact same way. You guys raised a darling. Chrysta isn't just beautiful but so smart and…" Terrence thought back to everything she'd told him when they met at the bistro. "*Driven.* She's so focused that she can do anything she puts her mind to. I don't think I've ever met someone so invested in succeeding that they're able to pick up just about anything and be good at it." These words were from the heart. He'd lay in bed at night just wondering how Chrysta managed to be so incredible. She wasn't aware, but he'd nicknamed her 'Wonder Woman' behind her back. If only they'd had more opportunities to meet this week. He might have had the chance to test the name in person.

The family nodded in agreement to his praise of Chrysta.

"She's always been like that." Danielle rolled her eyes fondly. "It made growing up with her a real pain."

"Oh yeah. Imagine being compared to someone at the top of their game in *every* aspect," Aliyah teased, gaining more chortles from everyone. She picked up her glass of orange juice with a brightening smile.

"It seems she's excelled at choosing a lover too." Their mother winked at Chrysta, who reacted with a tiny gasp of elation.

Terrence smiled.

That's why she wanted to have a fake boyfriend. She was used to being the star of the family.

He laughed. Of course, his girl wanted to be the best at this, too.

His girl.

He liked the thought.

"*Thank* you, Mom. You have no idea how much it means to hear you say that." Chrysta was over the moon for the little compliment. She bared her teeth at Terrence in a grin and happily ate the rice and peas on her plate. After using a napkin to dab her lips clean, she spoke up. "I was just lucky that Terrence came by when he did. It's so hard to find the right person these days that it's…"

As Chrysta continued, Terrence watched the sheer joy on her face grow more and more apparent. From sitting here and listening, he could tell that her family's opinion mattered deeply to her. The love she had for them was also palpable. While this was sweet, it also kind of worried Terrence that she valued their views so much. At the end of the day, people lived for themselves. What if she'd been truly content being single? Would Chrysta have gone to these lengths regardless? Through getting to know her these past few days, Terrence could tell she was open to sharing her life with someone. It was in the way that she talked about potential future plans. They'd had a few discussions on such via text, and Chrysta always spoke of living with someone she adored. Whether she'd be open to that person being him was another story.

"Okay, enough chit-chat. Show us the ring. Where have you been hiding it? The jig is up, Chryssie. We *need* to see that engagement ring!" Aliyah hooted and cheered to be shown the jewelry.

It was only at that point that Terrence realized they had no such thing! He tried not to panic in front of her family. "Oh, the ring?"

Chrysta looked up at him with wide eyes. He could almost hear her thoughts. She was pleading that he come up with a quick cover for this hiccup.

Chrysta's wish was his command. "It's…" Silence fell briefly as Terrence snapped his fingers as if trying to recall something. "It's still getting fitted." He flinched to show his embarrassment. "Sorry, when I first slipped it on her finger, we found out the band was too slack."

Chrysta seemed relieved. "Yes, but soon, I'll have a gorgeous ring for you guys to see." She mouthed a 'thank you' to Terrence and then continued eating. "So Aliyah—"

Her dad suddenly cleared his throat and sat back. He'd just finished everything on his plate. "You know, back in my day, a man had to *ask* the father of his girl to request her hand in marriage." He shook his head. "People just don't do that anymore. We need to go back to our roots." The man lightly tapped the table before laughing with Greg.

"So sorry, sir. With our relationship being secret, I simply couldn't." Had their situation been real, Terrence would have certainly asked him to marry her. He sort of felt like doing so now. It was true that Terrence hadn't known Chrysta for even a week, but somehow, his gut was sure of her.

He watched her profile as she laughed at more jokes told by her dad. Sewing had taught him the value of patience. Terrence never rushed into anything and often thought things through, but with Chrysta, something within the pits of his spirit just knew. *He* knew that she was the one. It might have been why she'd suddenly popped up in his life with such a unique situation. The heavens had sent him Chrysta.

If any friends of his had outlined his situation, saying that they'd fallen for someone within a few days, he may have called them crazy. But Terrence was certain he wasn't. It was just like his father always said; when a man knew, he knew. And that was Terrence's experience right now. Without a doubt, Chrysta was the one.

Now, he just had to figure out how to convince her to turn their fake relationship into a real one.

CHAPTER ELEVEN

"You were amazing." Chrysta smiled at Terrence, beaming with happiness. She was as bubbly as one could be after the evening that they had just had. Everything had gone according to plan, and she couldn't be happier. One could even say that Terrence's performance had been even more convincing than she'd bargained for. Every single person in attendance at her family dinner had been mystified by Terrence's confidence and smooth talking. Toward the end of their evening, Chrysta's dad had even invited him to look at his ship collection in the drawing room. This was something he only reserved for men he found respectable. She'd seen her father bring men from his workplace to the shelf designated for tiny warships he'd collected over the years all the time. Tonight, he'd invited her plus-one to observe, and that satisfied her.

Heck, for a minute, she had also believed that Terrence was her fiancé. His emotions had seemed so genuine, and her family's reaction was so warm and reciprocal... it had all just seemed so real.

That small, strange pit of longing in her yawned wide. It had felt real.

But it wasn't.

Terrence had just opened the door of his vehicle, ready to drive back to Peachwood. Chrysta's parents were still packing up inside, but after Terrence had assisted with some dishes, Chrysta's mom had ordered him home. Chrysta had agreed that Terrence should leave with his long drive in mind. Peachwood may have been a shorter distance away than Atlanta, but a forty-minute drive was still lengthy for nighttime. In Chrysta's mind, Terrence deserved to get some rest as soon as possible. He deserved it after acting so convincingly tonight.

"Thank you, Chrysta. I have to admit that it wasn't difficult to mesh well with your family," he said. The man was standing in the doorway of his car. Chrysta checked back quickly to make sure that they couldn't be overheard before turning back.

"You did great. Really. They genuinely like you." She smiled at him, but it felt a little more brittle than she meant it.

"Well, that's because I genuinely liked them. I had a lot of fun tonight with you and everyone. And honestly, if you hadn't pried me away from the dishes earlier, I'd still be in there talking soap operas with your mom."

Chrysta giggled as he laughed. What a lovely laugh he had. That and a welcoming smile. This man was certainly a blessing in her time of need. "Trust me, you don't have to do that. I'm sure there's housework awaiting you in Peachwood, so you have my permission to tend to it." She clasped her hands in front of her. It was pretty sad to say goodbye after such a great night, but she had to. "Thank you, Terrence." She stepped away from his car and onto her parents' fresh lawn. The night's air was crisp and fresh. Chrysta heard distant dogs barking and sprinklers fulfilling their roles as the neighbors snuggled within the walls of their houses. "Bye." She waved as he sat in the soft seat of his car.

Terrence shut the door and furrowed his brows. "It doesn't have to be goodbye for tonight."

Chrysta didn't understand what he meant. She arched her brow as Terrence revved his engine. "You've already done more than enough for me. I think it's only fair that you hurry back until needy old me requests your assistance again." She felt guilty enough as it was. He may have been sweet about this weird arrangement, but it didn't change how low she was making him stoop. "Please, Terrence. You don't have to—"

"It's not necessarily about what I feel like I *have* to do to convince anyone but what I'd *like* to do to celebrate a great night." Terrence put his hands on his steering wheel. He flashed Chrysta a perfect smile as the news broadcast of earlier replayed on his radio. "Chrysta, be my guest. Let's go have a drink at my place in Peachwood."

After everything he'd done, Terrence was inviting *her* over for drinks? Was he some kind of angel? "Oh, Terrence, I couldn't. I should be the one treating you to something spectacular." Chrysta folded her hands sheepishly, looking away with a brief laugh. "In fact, I think I *will* treat you."

"Chrysta, Chrysta…" Terrence stopped her gently. His tone was so calm. Chrysta couldn't resist looking at his deep brown eyes. "Don't forget who *volunteered* to help you out with all of this."

She was reminded of his willingness and grew bashful. "Okay, I guess a little drink is due then."

"Excellent!" Terrence laughed. "But it's only if you're up for it. If you've had a long day and need to rest, then that is *completely* under-standable."

She walked around his car and opened the passenger seat. From there, Chrysta hopped in and strapped up. Terrence's car was low but very comfy. It held her dearly like a tender embrace. "Please. That perfect dinner gave me enough energy to keep going until midnight," Chrysta said. "As long as you're okay with driving me back, I'm completely open to celebrating at your house."

Terrence's eyes lit up with delight. "That's the spirit." He pulled into the street, driving away from her parents' house while honking his horn.

"Terrence!" She laughed. "What's the deal?"

"Just continuing the celebrations since that's what we're doing!"

Chrysta noticed her mother's face in the kitchen window as they rolled out. She waved before sitting back. It'd been a while since she'd sat down to enjoy a smooth ride. Terrence's car seemed perfect for that. There were no hitches in the way that it moved. "Again, thank you."

"I *insist* that you don't mention it, okay? Like I said, I had fun." Terrence changed the station, and music was now playing. "I'm honestly having a great time getting to know you under these peculiar circumstances." He rolled up the windows and turned on the heat. The nights were getting cold, so she appreciated this.

"You have no idea how happy I am that you do." She held the strap of her seatbelt. "So what drinks are we having? Do they come with light snacks like cheese and crackers?" she asked teasingly.

Terrence chuckled. "You'll see when we get there. Though I'm pretty sure you'll like what I bring out. You strike me as an old wine sort of gal." He smirked at her.

How did he know? Chrysta asked herself. With little space between them, her questions came out louder than she'd intended. Terrence *definitely* heard and was laughing at her phrasing. "Sorry. I didn't mean to say that."

"I think you did. You just didn't mean for me to hear," Terrence pointed out. "And I just had a feeling. A feeling that happened to be right." He drove into a lane that would lead him out of her neighborhood. "Which means that you'll love what I've got in store for you this evening."

Chrysta got excited. "Okay. I guess I'll have to see for myself."

She was definitely looking forward to learning more about what Terrence had planned.

⚬❦⚬

Cozy was the word Chrysta thought after stepping foot in Terrence's humble abode.

"Home sweet home," he called in that melodic, happy voice. He led the way into the narrow kitchen door and brought his briefcase to the living room next door.

She was enchanted by the scent of rosemary emanating from the small table sitting at the heart of the dining room. Her childhood home had the same arrangement. The kitchen and room for dining functioned the same. "Home sweet… home." She walked slowly into the space and admired what she saw. It felt very lived-in and comfortable. As she stepped toward the cupboards, a snuggly sensation swaddled her shoulders. It was like a hug from someone distant trying to reach her. "Nice." There were oven mitts for every season hanging on the cupboards beside the silver sink. From Terrence's refrigerator to the stove close to it, it seemed old-fashioned. Did he have a certain aesthetic he preferred, or was this house not entirely his?

"The living room is nice, too," Terrence said on his way back in. He closed the door they'd come in through before opening a cupboard holding wine above the fridge. "Don't be a stranger, Chrysta. You have my permission to explore." He pulled down two bottles and rested them on the counter.

Chrysta felt like she'd been yanked out of a dream when he addressed her. "Thanks. I just love the ambiance of your kitchen." She indicated the oven mitts. "Were these handmade?" She wouldn't put it past the tailor to sew his own oven mitts.

"Yes, they are." Terrence held two wine glasses he'd gotten from the cupboard. "But not by me." He rinsed them at the sink, which had a window over it. The curtains hanging in front of it had a unique touch about them, too.

Surprised, Chrysta contemplated asking who'd designed them but stopped herself. Perhaps she could make an inference on her own.

Or, maybe it wasn't something that he wanted to share.

Either way, she'd wait for him to tell her as opposed to prying. "I love them." She'd leave it at that for now. As he accepted her compliment, she wandered slowly into the small living room. There was a staircase close by that led to another floor of mysteries, no doubt. Terrence may have said to venture out, but she'd stick to one floor.

She stroked the back of the couch sitting in front of the TV and walked slowly to the recliner next to it. A wooden rocking chair looked lonely on the other side of the sofa. The whole setup seemed empty, in her opinion. This home certainly wasn't designed with one person in mind. Did Terrence's parents live here? Where were they?

"I hope you're a fan of red wine." Terrence walked out of the kitchen holding two quarter-filled glasses. "This brand has been on the shelf for years. It's a classic."

His voice sent tingles on her skin in the intimate setting. Being here was like visiting a cottage in the mountains. Somehow, thoughts of work and pleasing her family weren't able to penetrate her skull. Peachwood wasn't that far from Sweetgum, but Terrence's house and even his aura felt that way for sure. She… liked it. For the first time in a long time, Chrysta wasn't on edge. She just felt curious and a bit nostalgic in a way she never had before.

She felt relaxed. Like nothing in the world could bother her. Terrence made her feel that way.

It was really nice.

"Thank you." She accepted her glass and inhaled the sweet wine aroma. "Red wine has always been my favorite." As Terrence sipped his drink, she lowered her gaze to the table behind the couch. She'd been standing in front of it to observe. Framed pictures lined the surface in large amounts. As she looked closely at one with a happily married couple, Terrence spoke up.

"That's something we have in common." He stirred his drink delicately. "Though I wouldn't consider myself someone who's big on alcoholic beverages."

"I have to agree. It's a once-in-a-while sort of thing for me. But if you'd brought one of my sisters here, they'd say that I don't drink ever." Chrysta placed the cold rim of her glass against her lips. She sipped and savored the hot buzz it left on her tongue. "I was never that sort. I guess you could say I've played it safe my whole life." She shrugged.

Terrence licked his lower lip. "Was it because you had to or because you wanted to?"

The questions made her frown. "Because..." She saw brief glimpses of her past. How she'd turn down offers to go to parties for fear of disappointing her parents. Deep down, she'd been slightly intrigued by the prospect of letting loose, but it still wasn't who she was. Even if there'd been no restrictions, Chrysta knew she'd make the same choices. "I wanted to." She smiled sheepishly. "Sorry if you were expecting me to confess some deep desire to let loose and go wild, but I am just *not* that kind of person. I like to get the things I want in life. I'm pretty motivated to do things to that end, and I definitely sacrifice a lot of my playtime for work time. Lots of people find that boring, I guess. So, sorry if you were looking for a secret wild child."

Terrence laughed. "I'd be content either way. When it comes to you, I'm never disappointed with what I find out. To this day, I'm still in awe at your cooking skills."

Chrysta felt the blood rise beneath her cheeks. "You give me too much credit."

"I honestly don't. I still think that you need some kind of show or channel or *something* because you're honestly really talented," Terrence went on. "But you've revealed already that you're the type who's good at everything, so you'd need a channel for all of your other hobbies, too."

She truly appreciated his praise. "In a perfect world, I would, but as it stands now, I am just *way* too busy." And that was the end of that. "If you ask me, I think that a *lot* of people would be interested in watching how a dress shop like yours runs." Chrysta tapped her cheek in fake consideration. "The fact that it's in Atlanta makes it all the more perfect. Big city, small shop, hundreds of customers. How does their top tailor handle so many orders?"

Terrence belly-laughed at that one. He made her laugh, too. Standing here with him felt right to Chrysta. It was nice that she'd found such a nice guy to play the part of her lover. Who else would possibly be this willing *and* easy to talk to?

"I'll bring it up to the boss." Terrence walked past her with an almost empty glass. "Give me a second, okay? I'll be right back."

His cologne lingered after he went to the staircase and ran up with zeal. Why did he suddenly seem so eager? She once again got that excited feeling. Did he have a surprise for her? "The wine is surprise enough." Chrysta appreciated this lovely invitation and evening so far. Sometimes, it was good to step away from the life of hustle she led.

The framed photos tempted her once again. Chrysta lowered her chin to stare at one.

An older couple dressed in their Sunday best filled the space within the picture frame. They seemed to be beside a church and looked glad with one another. Not only did their age strike her, but also the fact that the man was in a wheelchair. The woman held its handles and smiled down at his face. In response, he looked up with a smile of his own. She'd never seen such pure displays of happiness.

Without thinking, she lifted the photo and stroked it. "Wow. These two..." This had to be what love looked like. She put down the picture in search of another. There were quite a few spread out behind the sofa, all telling the story of people who loved each other and who connected with each other.

Chrysta picked up a circular frame with not only the couple but a little boy standing between them. The boy looked at least eight years old, and the couple was younger. Once again, the man sat in a wheelchair. She'd initially assumed that he'd wound up in one due to growing older, but now, she wasn't so sure. Had he perhaps been born disabled?

"Beautiful, aren't they?"

Chrysta quickly put the picture back when Terrence popped up without warning. "Terrence. I was just..." She didn't mean to be invasive. "Who's beautiful? The couple?" She didn't need him to spell it out. Chrysta had already gathered who they were and why this house seemed so old-fashioned. A man like Terrence certainly wouldn't choose to design his home this way.

"Yes." Terrence strolled to her side and picked up the photo she'd put down. "Wouldn't you say they're beautiful together?" He looked captivated by the photo. Terrence made it face Chrysta but kept an eye on the old family portrait. "And then there's me in the middle, soaking up all of their good vibes." He laughed at his younger self.

She smiled at his nostalgia, but only for a moment. "What happened?"

Terrence stared at it silently, then put it back with the others. "My mom… passed in her sleep when I was in high school."

The air felt heavy as questions raced through Chrysta's mind. Her mouth moved, and eventually, she settled on something that felt kind but neutral. She didn't know him well enough to understand what his grief might need, but sympathy was always appreciated. "I'm so sorry, Terrence."

"Thank you. It was a long time ago, but her loss still hurts."

"Of course," Chrysta wanted to do more, but she didn't think it would be appropriate. Mostly, she wanted to know more, and her questions danced at the edge of her tongue. She felt tempted to ask them all at once but held back. She'd give Terrence room to decide how to approach this.

"It was sudden," he continued. "Sudden but not so surprising." Terrence crossed his arms and stared at the ceiling. He leaned back on the table after breathing out. "She was the type of person who tried to be everything to everyone. The best mother to me, the best wife to my dad, and also the best caretaker for him, too."

"She sounds wonderful," Chrysta murmured.

"She really was."

Chrysta glanced at another framed photo. This one was just Terrence's dad. It captured him from the waist up. She saw his resemblance to Terrence in this one. "She was taking on a lot by herself?"

"I don't want it to ever seem like my dad was a burden. He wasn't. He was always supportive, involved, and incredible to be around. My mom just wasn't the type to ask for help. Especially from people who saw our family as less than ideal." Terrence stroked the top of his head wearily. "I guess bottling things up from everyone and giving her all to those she loved became too much." He seemed distant while talking. "Once Mom passed, I gladly took on the role as Dad's caretaker." He locked eyes with Chrysta, seeming less lost in memories. "It's probably the most rewarding thing I've ever done, though at first, it put some strain on me." He picked up the picture she'd been admiring. "But through taking care of Dad, I got closer to him and developed a deeper appreciation for who he was. We were both grieving, so it felt great to bond and even brought me closer to Mom."

Chrysta couldn't look away from him.

"Honestly, it helped me to understand why they loved each other so deeply. I think that it was those years of helping Dad that taught me what true love was. They've always been an exemplary example of what couples should strive to be, but through carrying out Mom's daily routine with Dad, I truly understood them." Terrence put one hand in the pocket of his tailored pants. It seemed he always wore these when out.

"That really *is* beautiful," Chrysta whispered while he rummaged through his pocket. "So, your Dad…"

"Yes." Terrence retrieved what he wanted and hid it behind his back. "He passed a few years ago." The man mustered a smile despite recounting such sad news. "I imagine them holding hands across the rainbow bridge to soften the sting of what happened." He opened his hand to show Chrysta what he'd gotten. "Here. If you put this on, then we can sell the story better than before."

Chrysta wasn't at all expecting what was revealed to her. "Is that a ring?" She blinked, stunned at the shimmering gold band. "Where did you get this?" It seemed shinier than any piece of gold she'd ever seen. Chrysta picked it up between two fingers for a closer look. "Wow. Is this what you'd gone upstairs for? Did you just have a ring this beautiful lying around?" She felt like she'd stumbled into a fairytale. How could something so small shine so radiantly?

Terrence chuckled. "It's not just a strange coincidence." He gently plucked the ring from her grasp. "Here. Stretch your ring finger so I can put it on for you. It already looks like a perfect fit."

Chrysta did as was told with a giggle. "If it's not a strange coincidence, then…" The dots connected in her mind. "Wait. Is this your mother's?" Immediately, she drew back and held her own wrist.

She didn't want to take something so precious from him, especially if their relationship wasn't real.

Terrence paused by her sudden retraction. "I think you should wear it. Tonight, the only thing that raised questions for your family was your missing ring. If we don't get you one soon, then they're going to realize something's amiss." He seemed to believe that this made perfect sense.

After listening to the tragic story of his wonderful parents, Chrysta couldn't simply accept something so precious. "No. I can't just wear your mother's ring. Didn't your dad give it to her? You should put it back where it belongs. At least for memory's sake." She looked into Terrence's kind eyes. How could someone be so generous despite having endured such hardships? Was his heart made of gold as well?

"You don't understand." Terrence laughed as he spoke. "My mom *told* me to make good use of her ring if she wasn't around anymore." He took a look at the circular piece of jewelry. "I think that now would be a good opportunity to do that."

Could Terrence hear himself? "On a *fake* fiancé?" Chrysta seemed lost. "No, Terrence. You need to save that for someone you actually care deeply about. Someone special who stole your heart and deserves to wear what your sweet dad gave to your mom." She shook her head and stepped carefully away. "I know you're only doing this to fix the small problem we ran into tonight, but I just can't. I admire how quickly you think, though." She truly did. "We can just keep saying the ring is getting fitted."

Terrence didn't look satisfied with this explanation. "I'm pretty sure that someone will catch on if we keep using that excuse. It's already unusual that I proposed with an unsuitable ring." He inched closer. "I can tell that your mother especially is sharp. Don't you think she'll start to suspect us?"

Chrysta gulped as she imagined everything unraveling. It was embarrassing enough that she hadn't found someone compatible with her in all these years, but what was worse? Being single or being so desperate for people's validation that she got someone to act as her fiancé? If her mom sniffed out her lie, things were *bound* to get ugly. "I can just buy myself a fake gold ring. No need to whip out the big guns." Although, knowing her family, they'd catch wind of fake gold, too. People *loved* inspecting engagement rings. After one long look, they'd know hers was phony.

The man shook his head. "Why should you do that when I have a legitimate ring right here?" He smiled and lifted his mother's wedding band. "I know that to you, it feels like you're overstepping, but I think it's up to me what I use this for."

Chrysta thought on it a little longer. "Why are you being so nice about all of this? Are you actually this big-hearted?"

For the first time, he seemed uncomfortable. It was almost as if she'd called him out on something. Chrysta couldn't pinpoint why he'd frozen but was itching to hear his response. What was really going on with Terrence? Agreeing to do this and sending her flowers was enough. She didn't need him offering up his deceased mother's ring. This took things to a whole other level.

Terrence seemed to find his words. "It may have been an unconventional way to meet someone, but what can I say? I like you. You're one of the coolest people I've met in a while. It's not just about me being nice. It's about you, Chrysta. You've charmed me."

He winked, then gently took her hand. "So much that I'm now completely dedicated to the role as your fiancé. Please."

She glanced at the ring, then his sweet eyes. He'd made several points, and she saw why they made sense. Chrysta knew that his idea was foolproof. She couldn't resist. "Okay."

With that, Terrence slid the gorgeous ring onto Chrysta's finger. It didn't take much effort to fit snugly. In fact, one would say it was perfect. Had Terrence had this adjusted to her size, or did his mom just happen to have the same hands as she did?

"Wow." Chrysta held her hand to her face and looked at herself in the shimmering gold. "Have you been polishing it?"

"I may have done a bit of polishing before bringing it down here for you." Terrence looked amazed by how it appeared. "I'd say it looks like it was made for you, but I'm not sure I can." He took her hand.

Chrysta let him hold her to examine it closer. "Thank you, Terrence. I don't think I could ever repay you for being so generous." She almost felt like crying. Their situation might have been fabricated, but right now, she was getting a glimpse of what being proposed to felt like.

It felt good. More than good, even.

It felt amazing.

She smiled at Terrence. "Your dad had great taste."

"I know. And not just in rings. My mom was everything." Terrence's thumb rubbed Chrysta's fingers before he looked into her eyes. "I think I may have acquired that from him."

She wasn't sure what to think. Were these hints? It had been a while since she'd allowed a man so close. Chrysta considered herself versed in detecting attraction but, for some reason, couldn't tell with Terrence. He may have been getting into character with all these loving remarks, but there really was no need for such while they were alone. Did Terrence have something to tell her? Should she ask?

"What do you mean?" Chrysta's face was on fire as she pulled back her hand to stroke the dazzling ring he'd given her.

Terrence grew a wide smile and opened his mouth to respond.

It was at that point that Chrysta remembered how far from home she'd traveled. "Wait. What time is it?" If they'd been in a movie, a disk would scratch to ruin the moment. She checked the clock in the kitchen and gasped. "It's almost 10 p.m.! I know it's a Friday, but I still have to wake up early." She panicked.

"Relax, relax," Terrence held up his hands in a calming gesture. "Don't worry. If you're ready to head back, I'll drive you. I think we've celebrated enough for one night." He looked pleased. "And soon, we'll have more reason to celebrate once my mother's ring convinces everyone that we're the real deal." He held up his fist.

The invite to fist-bump changed Chrysta's mind. Terrence couldn't possibly have seen her as anything else. She knocked her fist against his with a smile. "Right." She began to make her way out but stopped in the kitchen doorway. "Wait. You were saying something."

Terrence just brought their empty glasses to the sink. He slowed down at her back. "I was?"

Had he forgotten? If so, then her suspicions may have been correct. Terrence would have remembered if he'd wanted to confess. "Never mind. It's late." The exhaustion of being anxious about her family's reaction finally caught up to her. "Thanks again." She hopped down the short flight of stairs and led the way to his car parked in the yard.

The following week, Terrence was helping Aliyah and the bridesmaids with another fitting, lingering to try and get a hint of what Chrysta might be thinking about him. If anyone knew, it was probably her sister, right?

He was hoping to get more information from Aliyah, but he kept shooting glances at Chrysta from across the room, hoping to get more insight into how she was feeling.

That, or he just wanted to look at each other.

He placed a pin in a seam quickly, reflecting on his missed opportunity to tell Chrysta how he felt about her. Last Friday night would have been perfect to let her know his true feelings, but she'd cut him off. Instead of persisting and following up, he had let it go.

And now, he wished that he hadn't.

"This looks *so* perfect I might explode from happiness," Aliyah gushed. She turned around stiffly in front of the changing room's mirror that afternoon. Today was the final fitting day for the wedding. She'd arrived with everyone in her bridal party about an hour ago.

A couple of other tailors aided Terrence in inspecting what he'd made. About two were bending in front of the mirror near Aliyah to ensure things fit.

Terrence fixed Danielle's sleeve carefully and stepped aside to watch her reflection. There were mirrors all over this changing room. They were in the main one as opposed to the one behind the sewing quarters. This room had a runway of its own, but the ladies stood on flatter ground to be inspected.

"It's so perfect. I'm not the one getting married, yet I feel like a princess." From Terrence's understanding, the woman who spoke was Greg's sister. She spun in her dress and snapped photos in the mirror.

"There we go, that will work then." Terrence smiled at Danielle and Greg's sister. Finally, he had an excuse to move on, and he left Danielle to see about Chrysta. She seemed the least talkative out of all the happy ladies. His inference was that she simply wasn't as close to them as they were to each other. He hadn't known her long, but Terrence had picked up quite a bit about Chrysta. Serious, serious Chrysta. She seemed more delighted to advance her own skills than to get to know people. This was something he both admired and worried about. Could being that focused be considered a flaw?

He didn't really think so, but he could see how, with her sisters, that was a difficult place to be.

"Don't get too sidetracked." Chrysta's words pulled him back to reality. "Sometimes it feels like you're playing your role a little *too* convincingly." She smiled at him just as he realized he'd been staring.

Terrence felt embarrassed. "Oh. Sorry. I just think—"

"Oh, looks like the love birds are having a secret conversation." Aliyah laughed after turning around to face them. Greg's sister and Danielle did the same. "I still can't believe you've been dating someone and even got engaged in secret this whole time, Chryssie." She cocked her head to the side. "It almost doesn't seem real."

"I *know.* If we'd chosen a different tailor to fit us for the wedding, would we have just *never* heard of this secret engagement?" Danielle's brows were furrowed.

Greg's sister laughed. "I guess they would have gotten married in secret, too? Maybe you guys would have only found out about Terrence once Chrysta got pregnant." She crossed her arms while looking at Chrysta. "Was that your initial plan? To only surprise everyone after the first baby was conceived?"

Chrysta smiled, the movement a little brittle and sad, as they all giggled.

Terrence watched in silence as Chrysta responded. "That's not what would have happened," she said. "Come on, guys. I would have at least let you know before the wedding. We were just…" Chrysta faced Terrence. "We're both private people."

"Private when it comes to your own family?" Aliyah walked up to Chrysta with her hands on her hips. "You've always been a funny one, Chrys, but this whole situation is still throwing me for a loop." She gestured to Terrence, who smiled. "How could you have this hunk of a man just lying around and *not* show him off?"

Chrysta laughed. "Lying around? What is he? A piece of cake?"

"You know what she means." Danielle got closer as she unzipped the back of her dress. It seemed Terrence's assistants were through with examining their dresses. "If *I* had a Terrence, I'd never stop boasting." She tapped her cheek while staring into Terrence's eyes.

Terrence wasn't sure where this was going. "Well, you could say Chrysta's different. You would know better than most people as her sister." He wrapped his arm around Chrysta's shoulders.

Danielle narrowed her eyes. "It's almost as if Terrence just suddenly appeared. Like seriously. How do you hide a man this gorgeous, Chrys?"

"It's impossible," Aliyah frowned, stroking her chin. "Unless…" She looked upward.

Terrence heard when Chrysta gulped anxiously. He decided that this was enough speculation for one day. "All right, guys, cool down." He slid his hand across Chrysta's back before rubbing it down her arm to hold her hand. "The real reason Chrysta kept me a secret is a secret in and of itself." He held his finger to his lips.

Chrysta seemed lost by his statement, but her sisters looked fooled. Terrence winked down at her to ensure that she didn't give away that he was improvising.

"What do you mean it's a secret itself?" Aliyah held her hips. She gasped. "Is it because she wanted to surprise us? It's still weird that you kept your mouth shut so long, Chrys. Who does that?" She crossed her arms and cocked her head sideways.

Chrysta cleared her throat and hooked her arm in Terrence's. The sensation made him die, soar to the heavens, and then come back to his body. "Hey, don't put words in my mouth. Terrence didn't give the reason yet." She stared up at him like an expectant kitten.

He could at least pat himself on the back for alleviating her anxiety. With him here, Chrysta had nothing to worry about. He'd defend her till kingdom come if he had to. "It has more to do with you girls than you would think." Terrence could see the curiosity bursting from Danielle's eyes. Even Greg's sister was invested.

"I thought she just didn't like involving other people in her life. Aliyah, didn't you say Chrysta has always been..." Greg's sister looked contemplative as she thought of a word. "Standoffish?"

"What?" Chrysta's jaw hung open as she faced her sister.

Uh-oh, thought Terrence as Aliyah rushed to defend her choice of words. He hadn't intended for things to go south. Was it safe for him to keep intervening? The bickering between Chrysta and Aliyah was more playful than toxic. They acted like siblings fighting over whose turn it was to hold the remote. He guessed that even as adults, sisters fought.

"Guys, not in the dress shop, come on." Danielle broke them up by squeezing her lean body between them and pushing both ladies apart. Greg's sister snickered to the side with her cell phone out. The light from her camera shone radiantly.

Terrence took Chrysta by the shoulders and guided her to his hip again. "Be careful what words you say, Aliyah." He saw Chrysta making a cutting motion at her neck to Aliyah, who pulled silly faces. "And I was going to say that Chrysta kept us a secret so when you girls came in the other day, I could listen in on your conversation without your knowledge. She wanted me to get an inside scoop on what you guys were gossiping about while she wasn't around."

The joke landed well and caused the ladies to chuckle. They flicked their wrists and dismissed this silly explanation before deciding to change. As they left the room to get their clothes, Chrysta sighed with apparent relief.

"Thank you," she said with clasped hands. "Aliyah may not come off as the sharpest or most focused, but when there's a mystery, she tends to be the first one to discover the truth. For a while, I've been up at night praying she wouldn't put the pieces together." The elegantly dressed lady rubbed her arm while holding down her head. She eventually looked up at Terrence in what appeared to be gratitude. "So, thank you for throwing her off."

Terrence fixed the sleeve of her dress by straightening it. He marveled at how the aqua-blue piece flowed off her body like a sparkling river down a mountain. She'd never looked better. "Like I keep saying, don't mention it." He looked into Chrysta's eyes. "The last thing I want is for my soon-to-be fake wife-to-be uncomfortable. I'll always come to your rescue. Just say the word. In fact, you don't have to say a thing." He drew near until there was barely any space between them.

Chrysta seemed charmed. "I appreciate it," she said softly with his body close to hers.

Terrence caught himself leaning in and had to step away. He couldn't overstep. It may have felt natural to him, but Chrysta hadn't given any signs that she had returned his feelings. "You look beautiful, by the way."

Her brows crinkled until she looked down at the lovely gown on her body. "Oh, thanks. You know," she held the skirt open. "I was worried it wouldn't suit my figure, but now that I'm in it, I see that I had nothing to worry about." The beautiful woman grinned with almost a childlike wonder in her eyes. "I guess you really are the best at your craft. You made it fit perfectly in just a few days. I know you always say not to mention it, but thanks, Terrence."

Terrence would confess that he loved the words 'thank you' in her melodic voice. All words were songs when stated by Chrysta. The term 'music to my ears' had never felt more literal. He'd always called people who used it corny, but now, here he was, hearing tunes whenever Chrysta spoke. "I try. I do try."

A stint of silence fell between them.

"I guess I better go change." Chrysta moved one of her twists to the back of her ear. He'd never met a woman who rocked every conceivable hairdo so effortlessly. Did she know how stunning she was? He adored how each neat twist dropped past her ears in shiny strands. "See you later, Terrence."

"Yeah. See you." Terrence leaned in and pecked her cheek before she left.

Chrysta touched her face before smiling and heading off.

He hoped she didn't mind his small showings of affection. It was hard to be around her and not express his feelings. He was going to tell her. But the timing wasn't right at the moment. "See you later." Terrence smiled to himself as she left through the passageway to exit the room.

CHAPTER THIRTEEN

From the elegantly styled red attire to the white decorations, everything for Aliyah's bachelorette party had gone exactly as planned. All attendees looked absolutely stunning, and they'd had a grand time eating finger foods and telling stories around Aliyah's living room. The photos snapped by the hired photographer truly captured the tame, womanly ambiance of the amazing evening.

Chrysta would have loved it if they'd left tonight at that and called it Aliyah's graduation from her days as a wild child, but no. It simply wouldn't have been practical to expect her cantankerous sister to settle for such a mild evening as her last night single. So, when Aliyah's friend Claudette had turned up near midnight with news that the party bus was 'here and ready' to take them to Atlanta, Chrysta shouldn't have been as surprised as she had been.

But heading into the big city with her sister's rowdy friends wasn't exactly how she wanted to spend her evening.

"Okay, everyone, say bachelorette party part two!" Aliyah used a selfie stick to snap a photo of everyone bunched in the backseat. The bus was *huge* and lived up to its name. While the outside was sparkling pink, the inside reminded Chrysta of what she'd seen musicians travel in on tour. Through the door was a long hallway lit up with bright purple lights and a long seat on either side. The very back seat was your typical backseat of a bus. The driver blasted dance-pop hits to which Aliyah, her friends, and Danielle danced. Everyone had started off on one side of the bus but wound up changing places during the course of the drive. They'd been driving for almost an hour, and yet, the energy levels were still through the roof.

"Girls, when we get there, we are going to *rock out!*" said Claudette with a martini. The bus had a cooler behind the driver's seat with drinks of all sorts.

As everyone cheered, Chrysta clapped. This section of the party had apparently been orchestrated by Danielle as a surprise for Aliyah. Their mom had initially been present but left before the 'shenanigans'—as she called it—took place. Right now, Greg's sister, Chrysta's sisters, and all of Aliyah's friends filled the bus to capacity. Despite the bus's fast motions, every woman would stand now and then to dance.

Chrysta had only heard of her sister's wild adventures but had never tagged along for any. In just about thirty minutes, they'd be popping champagne bottles at a strip club. This would *surely* be interesting.

"I don't want anyone not getting on that dance floor and losing their absolute *minds,* okay?" Aliyah just got up to hold one of the poles in the pathway. She hadn't had any drinks but was still on top of the world. "Chrysta, do you hear me? You have to go crazy tonight. Don't worry about work or any of your other responsibilities."

Chrysta rolled her eyes as the bubbly women laughed.

"Yes. Tonight is all about going completely insane. So, have as many shots as you can. Every drink is on Claudette." Danielle grabbed Chrysta's arm as the others encouraged her to let loose. "It's Friday night, after all. You don't have anywhere to be tomorrow. At least not anywhere important."

So far, Chrysta was the only one besides Aliyah who hadn't had a drink. She'd taken enough beverages at part one of Aliyah's party. In her eyes, there was no need for others. Especially not foreign ones set up by Aliyah's friend. Why hadn't Aliyah had anything? She would normally be the first to start downing anything alcoholic. Chrysta supposed she'd drink when they got there. "I understand the spirit of having fun, but the last thing I want to do is not be aware of my senses so far from home. For that reason, I'll dance and have a good time *but* without consuming too much," she said slowly to the disappointed women.

Danielle scoffed. She spun around the stripper pole with rolling eyes. "Good luck trying to find a drink with no alcohol in it over there. You're *bound* to get thirsty." She laughed along with the others. "I'm kidding." She nodded at Claudette, who'd taken a seat to eat the cherries in her drink. "Did you organize free non-alcoholic beverages for us? Chrysta's agreed to be responsible tonight, as usual. I mean, at least *one* of us should be, and I'm glad I can count on my big sister to be that person!"

"Yes. Better you than me. Chrysta can be everyone's big sister!" Greg's sister put down her canned beer before patting Chrysta's back.

Claudette swallowed a cherry and put her glass on the floor. With all the motions, Chrysta didn't understand why she'd put that there. "Of course." She flipped some of her bright pink braids off her shoulders. "Just check out the sodas. They're fine. In our VIP section, they'll be the bubbly drinks that the waiters are serving." She had to shout over the lively music.

"Bubbly drinks? What color?" Chrysta could see them rising to dance again. It seemed their driver had cranked up the tunes.

"Ladies, we are almost to our destination!" the man announced into a microphone. His voice boomed from the surrounding speakers. "Let's have one more dance-off for the road, shall we?"

Chrysta whipped her head around as everyone cheered and

started bumping and swaying. "Claudette!" She got up and held a pole of her own.

Claudette was already clapping for Aliyah, who danced wildly and with an equal mix of talent and abandon on a pole.

Chrysta called her again, and she finally faced her. "What color are we talking for these drinks?"

Claudette put her hands up and bumped her hips. "Transparent. But don't worry about that. Dance!" She grabbed Chrysta's hands to invite her to join them. "Chrysta's going to do something before we stop. Show us your best move, Chryssie, baby!"

The other ladies chanted with passion to encourage her.

Chrysta would have backed out on every other night, but downing people's moods wasn't her style. "Okay, fine." She kicked off her heels and attempted some tricks on the pole. The screaming that followed was unmatched.

But it was also kind of satisfying.

She liked that her sisters were a little shocked right now and that they couldn't believe what was going on. She was more than just the DD.

She was a person, too. And she also contained multitudes.

Including, apparently, a party girl.

INSIDE THE CLUB was a world of its own. Their upbeat bus paled in comparison to this realm of fun and parties. The central dance floor lit up in different colors, and so did the stage and bars. It felt wide enough for at least a thousand people. The upper floors were swarming with them. Just like any strip club would, this one contained talented women performing acrobatics on sparkly poles.

Chrysta clapped and danced with the rest of Aliyah's party. Claudette had requested VIP treatment for them, so currently, they had a section for themselves. They congregated at a small square by the dance floor with fancy seats and its own waiters. Red stanchion separated them from regular club goers. Servers went in and out of the blocked area with snacks and drinks of all manner.

"You said the transparent, fizzy ones were non-alcoholic?" Chrysta asked above the ear-popping tunes. The colorful lights and spectacles were something out of a dream. Not her dream, but she was sure that out there, this was *someone's* fantasy come to life.

Claudette lifted a glass of something pink off a tray. "Ooh, those are the sodas. Great choice, Chrysta!" She rammed her hip into Chrysta's, then proceeded to dance energetically. They'd already taken turns throwing cash at the performers, but Aliyah was on her way forward to try again.

"How are sodas a great choice?" Chrysta asked herself after pausing. She didn't know about them, but her feet were getting tired. The heels she wore made them ache. All the dancing and laughing had been fun, but now, she was running low on juice. Her mouth especially was dry from staying far from drinks. Those she'd seen so far didn't interest her. It was only a while ago that she'd caught wind of something non-alcoholic.

"Here you go, ladies." Yet another server slipped in with a tray of short glasses. They were clear and bubbly, like what Chrysta held in hand.

She downed the contents of her soda to reach for two more glasses. "Thank you," Chrysta said. She drank what was in them and put them back on the tray. "It kind of burns, but at least it's refreshing," she said to no one as the waiter carried on. Everyone took what they wanted and went on with their night.

To think, right now, Terrence was probably in a similar position. Caught up with several guys who wanted nothing more than to party. She didn't know why he came to mind, but he did. It may have been last minute, but Terrence had received an invite to Greg's bachelor party. Chrysta supposed it made sense since he was his fiancé's sister's partner, but it felt sudden. She supposed it had a lot to do with Chrysta herself randomly dragging Terrence into their lives. What would everyone say if they found out? In truth and in fact, Terrence was just a stranger doing a favor.

She slowed down her dancing to look at her ring. Would a stranger pass down something so beautiful to her? And what about the time he came to her defense? Once in a blue moon, unknown people would speak on others' behalf, but in Terrence's case, it was different. Yes, it hadn't been long since this bogus arrangement came to be, but he already felt closer than some of her family. It might have been his soft kisses or constant check-ins that made him feel close, but whatever it was, Chrysta adored it. She actually wished he was here. Would Terrence appreciate this extravagant club and all the wild dancing? He seemed like the type who'd blend in just fine. Meanwhile, Chrysta was having trouble staying on her feet.

She pushed aside the laughter from everyone around her to find a place to sit within their stanchion barricade.

After sitting on a white cushioned seat, Chrysta kicked off her heels. "That feels so good." The relief was astounding. She wore heels to work and to important engagements, but dancing in them was a whole other ball game. Once she'd recharged on bare feet, she'd hop back into the fun and games.

"Drink?" The same server returned with his tray almost empty. He held it near Chrysta and waited.

She could use another refresher. Beverages and meals always tasted better while sitting. "Thank you." Chrysta drank the cold glass of soda and then placed it back on the tray. She wiped her mouth with the back of her palm as everything became wonky.

Aliyah came racing back to their area with her phone out. "I got so many pictures and videos! I feel like I'm a celebrity at a huge party or something. This is amazing!" She squealed with a few of her tipsy friends, then spotted Chrysta. "Chryssie, why are you sitting down? You should come with me to get a better look at the action."

Chrysta saw Aliyah strutting toward her, but her sister's image was sideways. "Ally?"

Aliyah sat heavily beside her. "It's like I'm in a music video!" She showed Chrysta her phone. "That's me throwing all the money at them. I even put on my sunglasses. It was great! Danielle got everything so perfectly." Her head began to turn. "Where is she? Danielle? Danielle!" She waved her hand dismissively. "She's probably sick somewhere." Aliyah put her phone away. "She is *such* a lightweight! She didn't even have that many shots."

Just then, Claudette came dancing up to them with two other friends and a server with *yet* another tray of drinks. "Did someone say shots?" She clapped over her head as the girls and even their server squealed.

Everything got swirly to Chrysta, like she'd just stepped off a merry-go-round. She couldn't think straight, and her limbs were unreliable. "I'll... pass." She hiccuped and covered her mouth. "Where are we again?" Her judgment was suddenly non-existent. There was so much music and cheering, but somehow, she couldn't recall what it meant. She kind of wanted to join the fun but knew something was amiss. "Is the soda... *hiccup...* did the soda do this?" Her tongue was like a weight in her mouth.

"Say cheese!" Aliyah took photos as her friends drank with glee. "What did you say, Chrysta?"

Chrysta saw everything zooming in and out. She hiccuped again. "The soda is crazy over here." She blinked at Claudette. "You said the soda was crazy."

Claudette furrowed her brows and sat beside Chrysta. "What sodas? The lime soda or the vodka soda?"

The word 'vodka' made Chrysta's heart jump. "*Vodka* sodas?" she slurred. No wonder she felt so strange.

She was drunk.

"I saw you taking a bunch of them just now. I told you they were a good choice." Claudette grinned. "Oh wait." It seemed something suddenly clicked for her. "You said you weren't drinking tonight." She gasped and covered her mouth.

For a second, only the beat and laughter from the dance floor were audible.

Their silence was cut short by Chrysta laughing heartily. Her passionate laughter invited Aliyah and her girls to laugh with her, and they did so for an uncomfortably long time.

"I have to text Terrence. I have to. I have to," Chrysta said with joyful tears draining from her eyes. She stuffed her hand in her purse as her body jerked with hiccups. "I have to." She kept repeating the same line while Aliyah and her friends retold the absurd situation for more laughs. Deep down, Chrysta knew this wasn't funny but couldn't react appropriately due to her intoxicated state.

She swiped through her contacts in search of her fiancé and tried to keep her head straight. Did she have a reason for contacting Terrence, or was this just the alcohol talking? They *were* together, after all. Just like Aliyah and her friends, Terrence may just get a kick out of this story. He deserved to have a good laugh.

"On a scale of one to ten, how drunk is she?" This person just approached their seat. It was Greg's sister who carried her heels in her hands. She seemed eager to keep partying but stopped by to check on them. It seemed Aliyah had just relayed Chrysta's hilarious predicament to her.

Aliyah waved her hand quickly in front of Chrysta's face, making her dizzy. "I'd say a six. Chrysta, do you understand anything I'm saying?" She scratched her head. "She's not the 'get drunk' type, so I have no idea how to gauge this. She could be a ten, but I'd have no idea."

As Greg's sister brought up the possibility of leaving early for Chrysta's sake, their voices took on an echoey quality. Chrysta lifted her eyes away from her cell phone and stared past Greg's sister's body. The dance floor was there, glowing like a collection of stars in a vibrant sky. Music pounded her skull and made everything vibrate. She wasn't sure if she despised or hated the things happening right now, but more and more, she lost her grip on reality.

"Terrence…" He *needed* to know about this crazy night. Why was he, of all people, stuck in her mind right now? Were they really together?

Just then, she remembered their wacky arrangement and vowed to her intoxicated self to not let anything spill. By all means, she *had* to keep herself aware enough to maintain their secret. Who knew what Aliyah would do if she found out?

"Who are you calling?" Claudette was suddenly close to her face.

Chrysta could feel the cold screen of her cell phone against her cheek. Had she dialed a number? "I… gotta go…" The words rolled off her tongue like a bowling ball. She got up without thinking and left before things got ugly. Chrysta could deduce that she'd called Terrence since she'd been searching for his contact but wasn't sure why.

As she staggered through dancing bodies, her senses became shrouded by the power of alcohol. Before she knew it, she had lost control, and things were pitch-black. The only thing she knew was that Terrence had answered.

Then, nothing.

CHAPTER FOURTEEN

Ten minutes earlier.
Ping!

His ball hit another and sent it straight into the hole. Terrence stood taller as applause rolled in from his fellow guests. He held his pool stick like a cane as they clapped in admiration.

"Wow, Greg. Where did you get this guy? His pool skills are off the charts." A friend of Greg's left the couch in the man-cave to high-five Terrence. The man's other hand held a can of beer he'd been sipping for five minutes. Should it run out, there were plenty of others to choose from. This sanctuary for men had a mini fridge in its small kitchen attached to the main room. Not only was there a pool, foosball, and air hockey table, but also a humungous flatscreen hanging high on the wall. Terrence had even spotted a Jacuzzi in the corner. There'd been one upstairs in the living room, too. Greg's house was certainly the largest one Terrence had visited in a while.

Greg seemed proud to have invited him. He, too, placed the tip of his pool stick on the ground before answering. "How many times do I have to tell you? He's my fiancé's sister's secret fiancé." He walked around the table to grab Terrence's shoulder. "Not sure why she kept him secret, but I'm glad she revealed him just in time for the bachelor party." He winked at Terrence as they laughed.

"Right, right. And I must say that I'm flattered that you invited me." Terrence touched his chest to indicate sincerity. He definitely hadn't anticipated this at all. Out of the seven guys here, he only knew one and had met Greg about a week ago at dinner. To say he'd been intimidated by the invite would be an understatement. Luckily for Terrence, he was pretty good at making friends. From the moment Greg had led him to the basement, he'd started cracking jokes with the other guys lounging around the area. They'd welcomed him pretty warmly with handshakes and had invited him to take whatever he wanted from the fridge and pantry. Within minutes, Terrence had blended right in with them.

As far as bachelor parties went, this one was laid back. Most of Greg's friends just sat around with drinks and snacks. A hockey game that many of them were engrossed in was on TV. They seemed transfixed by the events happening on screen and would pop up to cheer when a score was made. Three guys were currently in the kitchen having snacks and sharing anecdotes from their time in college. Around the pool table was just Terrence, Greg, and this guy named Devon. He'd gotten up from his spot on the couch to watch.

"You don't have to be flattered." Greg patted Terrence's back. "We're family. We're marrying two sisters. That makes us brothers-in-law. It only made sense to ask you over, given that we'll be seeing a whole lot of each other for the rest of our lives." Greg laughed. "Don't act all shy and flattered. You've been a *treat* to have around."

Terrence appreciated the compliment. He lowered his gaze to the table of balls while thinking back to Chrysta. Their situation wasn't what everyone thought, but they sure had convinced people. All of this integration into the family and talks of marriage was putting him in the mood. Which, of course, meant the mood for settling down and spending the rest of his life with someone.

Not just someone, either.

With Chrysta.

Her family was sweet; they liked him, his mother's ring fit *perfectly* around her finger, and she herself was everything he'd ever wanted in a partner. If those reasons didn't mean they should date, then Terrence didn't know what did.

There was one fairly pretty major problem. While his feelings were genuine, he wasn't sure if hers were. Terrence would be happy to marry Chrysta for real.

If only she liked him back.

He could tell she was fond of him and appreciated his affection, but he still wasn't sure if Chrysta *loved* him. Terrence knew for sure he'd fallen for Chrysta, but she may not reciprocate his feelings. And, of course, the only way that they could make their fake engagement a reality was for Chrysta to return his feelings. His heart would shatter if he confessed and somehow scared her in the process. He was embarrassed just thinking of the potential disaster.

His ring tone suddenly blared from his phone speaker.

Greg and Devon had started discussing the complexities of pool while Terrence had drifted into thought. They both paused when his phone overpowered their conversation. "It's pretty late. Who's calling?" asked Greg with a smirk.

Terrence wasn't sure what that look meant but ignored it. "I don't know," he said. He slipped his phone out. One look at the caller ID explained everything… at least to Devon and Greg.

"The missus!" the two said. They hit Terrence's shoulders while saying lines like, 'Go get her, tiger' and 'Of course.'

Terrence smiled partially and put down his stick. He hurried up the stairs out of the basement and stood on the upper floor. Chrysta was supposed to be at Aliyah's party. Why call him in the midst of all her fun?

"Hey Chrysta. Everything all right?" Terrence wandered into Greg's spacious living room as the sound of club music came through the line.

"Terrence," Chrysta blubbered. She seemed to be either crying or speaking with a full mouth. "It's so loud, and I had too many sodas."

His brow went up at her almost incoherent words. What was going on? "Too many sodas?" The chatter and rhythm in the background allowed him to piece together what may be the case. Though Terrence didn't exactly pin Chrysta as the type to lose control this way. "What sodas?" Was she in trouble? Perhaps lost and confused? "Where's Aliyah?" His curiosity switched to concern.

"She's there with everyone, but I had to call you. I got so drunk, and I'm so drunk, and you were the first thing in my brain like a toaster. You popped in my head like toast or something like a toaster."

Chrysta was rambling. He loved her cute internal dialogue, and he loved it even more now that it was specifically for him.

Terrence stopped in front of Greg's living room flat screen and scratched the back of his head. There were old family photos on the TV stand. He glanced at one with a young Greg and his mom before noticing another with the boy and his dad. "Toaster?" He smiled. Aliyah and the other girls were close, so she wasn't in danger—just drunk. Since she shared with him that she wasn't a big drinker, he knew that she was probably struggling a little right now. "How did sodas make you drunk, Chrysta?" He laughed and crossed one arm. "Did someone spike them?"

"They were vodka sodas, and I didn't know, but I thought about you, and I said you were my fiancé, but it's all a fake thing to make them think we're together, but for just a little bit, one second, I thought it was real." Chrysta's run-on sentences were difficult to keep track of, but he understood them. "And when I thought it was real, I was the happiest, but now it's, like, so sad because I literally love you, but it's not real."

Terrence froze for all of five seconds.

It was like everything, and everyone stopped to gasp at the same time the revelation sunk in. What was it his dad always said? A drunk mind spoke a sober heart? Had Chrysta just confessed to him?

"Woah," Terrence let a massive grin stretch across his face. His heart beat rapidly, and his chest fuzzed up. So Chrysta *did* feel the same. He couldn't imagine her possessing the capacity to lie like this. With her faculties in order, Chrysta spoke clearly and with purpose. Right now, her words were all over the place. The slurs were kind of cute and childlike, so he could tell she couldn't hold back. That had to mean that he wasn't alone. "You love me?" He'd ask again just to confirm. Sometimes, drunk folks just babbled.

"Yeah. I do. I love you a lot. More than any guy I've dated, and I don't even date you. It's not fair that we're just acting. Our romance is so good. Your mother's ring, your kindness. And your face, too. Terrence, you are so *hot*. The first time I saw you, I thought you were so hot, and you just keep getting hotter and *hotter.*"

Terrence laughed at her loss of control. Poor Chrysta. If only she could hear herself. There was no way she'd remember *any* of this conversation in the morning. He'd been in her position a couple of times in college. The only way he'd been made aware of his drunken escapades was through photos taken by friends. It always embarrassed him to know the sort of ridiculous antics he'd gotten up to. That was partially why he'd vowed to never get that drunk again.

The man took a seat on the arm of Greg's couch. It was leather and squeaked with sudden movements. "Thanks, Chrysta." But if there was a possibility that she'd never recall this conversation, this may be his chance to unveil his devotion. "I…" Why was he nervous? She'd spoken up first. He'd also just established she'd forget this all in the morning. "I think you're hot, too."

Chrysta inhaled sharply. *"Really?"*

He liked how flattered she sounded. "Yes. You're probably one of the most beautiful women I've ever laid eyes on." Terrence turned his head toward the stairs to the basement. He knew none of the other guys would use his gushing against him but still rather keep this conversation away from them. Just in case its direction caused him to reveal his and Chrysta's secret. "I've thought this way since the moment I saw you. You know that you're beautiful, don't you?"

She laughed, and it made him smile. This may have been the freest he'd heard her. Their interactions did come with instances where they chuckled and smiled, but he'd never heard Chrysta bellow this way. It was probably the sexiest thing Terrence had ever listened to. "I try to be beautiful. I do try. For myself, for my mom, and… for you too now since you're my fiancé. Oh, sorry; *pretend* fiancé."

Terrence saw an opportunity he couldn't miss out on. "If you want, we can erase the 'pretend' before fiancé and make things official." His heart ignited as sweet words filled his brain. "In fact, I'd actually been thinking of it for a while." He got up without thinking and strolled into the kitchen. It may have been his nerves moving him about. Terrence was collected in most cases, but Chrysta did something to him. "I somehow forgot to respond to your confession properly. I'm sorry." He stopped close to the sink and stared at the window. Greg's front lawn was a work of art. There was a concrete fence surrounding his dwelling and a gate attached at the front. What baffled Terrence more than its size was that this wasn't Greg's only house.

But that didn't matter now. He was in the middle of something phenomenal. "I should have said that I love you too because I really do, Chrysta. It hasn't been long, but I think I know how I feel."

"Terrence," Chrysta squealed. "You're being too nice. You love me, and I love you, so that means we *need* to get married for real. Everyone make way for Chystence!"

He had a good time laughing along with her. "In fact, I love you so much that I'd actually been planning on letting you keep my mom's ring after I gave it back to you the right way." He heard her celebratory squeaks dying.

"*Hiccup.* What do you mean?" Chrysta slurred.

"Well…" Terrence gave his back to the sink and leaned. "Do you remember when your dad said a man should ask the father of the woman he wants to marry before proposing to her?"

"My dad said all that? I don't remember, Terrence. *Hiccup.*"

"It was implied when I brought up our engagement. It's okay if you can't recall right now." His eyes settled on the pear-shaped napkin holder on Greg's dining table. There were four chairs around it. He imagined two parents and two kids sitting over dinner there. The parents were him and Chrysta. Of course, if they ever got to that stage, they'd live somewhere that *wasn't* Greg's abode, but his fantasy served to say he yearned for more with the intoxicated woman he spoke with. "Just know that after he said that, I'd planned on asking him for your hand in marriage before officially proposing to you with my mom's ring. Just so we do things properly for our *real* engagement."

Chrysta seemed completely enamored. *"Terrence."* Her girlish giggles were music to his ears. "You're so romantic! I loved the flowers you sent and all of your kisses, and now you're making me love you more with all this engagement talk. Terrence, you're so..." Chrysta went on and on and eventually drifted into speaking gibberish.

Terrence had to say he loved this lovey-dovey drunken Chrysta. He wished she'd be this open while sober. It shouldn't take substances to make her unwind. "Okay, Chrysta, I know. Thanks for all the sweet words, but we should end this call. I'm sure Aliyah still has a lot in store for your outing. I don't want to distract you from all the fun. Is she still close by?"

"There are people dancing everywhere, and I nearly bumped into one. I see her with the others. They're throwing cash at that pole lady. I guess I should sit. My feet are killing me, and I don't even know what's happening. It's like I'm on the moon or *hiccup* something."

"I can imagine." Terrence hoped and prayed that she was only drunk and not somehow high from a foreign substance. Aliyah seemed like the type to sprinkle enhancers in people's drinks. It wasn't that he distrusted her, but she just struck him as wild. "Go take a seat."

He waited until Chrysta reported she was sitting before hanging up.

For a while, all he did was smile while staring at the fridge. It was true what he said. He meant every word about proposing and requesting permission from her father. The thought made him anxious, but Terrence had to. Plus, it wasn't like they could deny him. As far as they knew, he'd already asked for her hand. Her folks also seemed to want what was best for her. He certainly had nothing to worry about.

CHAPTER FIFTEEN

It felt like just yesterday that Aliyah had introduced Greg to their family. Now, after tons of antics, a rushed lie, and the wildest night of Chrysta's life, the wedding was only one day away. By this time tomorrow, her middle sister Aliyah would be a married woman. Chrysta could hardly believe it.

"Just like old times, eh?" Danielle said after fluffing the pillow of her air mattress. For their little sleepover at their childhood home, they'd chosen Chrysta's room to crash in. Their parents were out at a charity dinner, so they couldn't stick around to bask in the nostalgia.

Chrysta put her phone on the board of her bed and looked down. Both Danielle and Aliyah seemed content on the floor. They'd dragged mattresses from their respective rooms to make themselves at home there. "Yes. Back when you two couldn't get enough of me." She dragged her bonnet from the knapsack she'd packed, then dropped it to the ground beside her bedside table. When they'd first come here, everything had felt so bare. The absence of her posters of outstanding women in business and collectible items on her dresser had left her deflated. Chrysta could describe the day she'd stored them away without much assistance but still expected to find them after returning to her childhood room.

It was only when Danielle and Aliyah had laid out their stuff and inflated their temporary beds that the room began to feel like hers again. They'd turned off the lights to watch movies in their pajamas and had brought snacks up from downstairs to munch on while gossiping. They'd kept it to a minimum, but she and Aliyah had had a few back-and-forth exchanges with one another during the course of the night. With her sisters here, personal items weren't necessary for her room to feel like home.

Aliyah tied her hair down and then crossed her legs. "You can't blame younger siblings for being obsessed with their older siblings. You were like the only example of how to be human for us back then. It was only natural that we'd follow you around." She took a deep breath. "Although even after Danny and I got old enough to think on our own, we'd still end up begging to sleep over in your room from time to time." She smiled at Chrysta. "Do you remember that?"

Chrysta did. Back then, she'd considered it a bother, but now, she kind of missed those days. She loved her sisters, and she loved her childhood, and she cherished those memories.

"And you'd always be so bossy about it. You'd spend the whole night saying things like 'Don't touch my books' and 'Stop talking' and 'Go to bed' instead of getting to know us better." Danielle crawled off the mattress to grab an uneaten packet of chips. She crept back into her spot and ate with no regard for the crumbs she may leave.

Not wanting to be a jerk, Chrysta held back from advising her to stop. It was just a shame that she'd already cleaned up after their last snack session. "Hey, I wasn't wrong. You two would always do that on a school night when we had to be up at five the next morning. I was only being responsible." She leaned against the wall beside her bed. "Plus, I would have been a bad example if I had stayed up to giggle with you two all night."

Aliyah rolled her eyes. "But that's not the point. Not *everything* has to be stiff and rigid." She flung her arms into the air. "Live a little sometimes! Even if you face the consequences, it's better to have stories to tell when you're older than to not." She snatched her pillow and squeezed it on her lap.

Danielle jabbed her thumb at Aliyah. "Take it from the queen of wacky stories." Her mouth was so full that Chrysta had trouble understanding her. "I sometimes tell Aliyah's high school stories as my own to seem cool to my coworkers."

That earned an all-out laugh from both Aliyah and Chrysta. When she was done, Chrysta shook her head and crossed her arms while the two younger ladies snickered. "Lying is *also* not okay, but whatever."

"Do you remember that time I got in trouble for writing my initials in lipstick on everyone's lockers for my birthday?" Aliyah held out her hand in a peace sign while Danielle sniggered.

It was hard to hold in her laughter, so Chrysta let loose. "That was *so* uncalled for and, quite frankly, humiliating on your part. It wasn't even like you were one of the popular girls that everyone would have been honored to get an autograph from, either. You just did that as an ordinary school goer that no one cared about." She could see their parents scolding Aliyah now.

Aliyah's mouth was agape. Meanwhile, Danielle laughed heartily with a mouth full of chips. "I was definitely popular. You just didn't know because you never kept up to date with who was who in school. All you cared about was maintaining good grades and telling people what to do."

"What about the time when you got in trouble for trying to 'stand up to the man' by demanding that teachers stop giving us homework?" Danielle wheezed on the bark of a laugh that followed.

Chrysta just shook her head while the two looked back fondly at Aliyah's wilder days. The wife-to-be hadn't changed much since then, but Chrysta did detect some level of maturity. At least her sister never acted out at work. For the most part, Aliyah behaved herself there as far as Chrysta knew.

Aliyah wiped tears away from both her eyes. "But at least you took a page out of my book for the party last night."

"I can't believe she recovered so fast from that *horrible* hangover." Danielle covered her mouth after stuffing it with food. "You must be a goddess to bounce back so quickly."

Chrysta shuddered once the memories of her awful spell of sickness came back to her. She'd awoken on Aliyah's couch this morning with a mega migraine and the urge to puke, which had overwhelmed all of her self-control very quickly. Not a trace of the events of last night had been present in her mind. The only reason Chrysta had even known her own name was because Aliyah had talked to her when she sat up. If her younger sister hadn't been around, Chrysta might have wandered out to inquire about her identity on the streets. "I consider it a gift from God because if I'd stayed sick past noon, I may have checked myself into a morgue." Her joke was well-received. "I'm just glad I didn't do anything humiliating while blackout drunk." If she had, Aliyah would have certainly captured it on video. The absence of embarrassing footage of herself put Chrysta at ease. It seemed no one had been fully conscious enough to record anyone's slipups. The most she'd seen were videos of everyone throwing it down under colorful lights.

Aliyah tsked. "I wouldn't speak too soon. The rest of us had been way too out of it to report anything or give an account. If something particularly insane happened, we may just get an update from some stranger on social media." She held her chest. "Believe me, it's happened. I usually give it a few days before I say I'm in the clear."

This information didn't help Chrysta's fears, but she appreciated the advice. "Thanks." It was rather kind of her sister to not only share her expertise on drunken outings but also to assist Chrysta during her *terrible* bout of sickness. Oddly, Aliyah hadn't shown any symptoms of being hungover, so she had been more than capable of nursing her to health. Over the years, they'd fought like dogs over the silliest things, but now, things had mellowed out. Was it because Chrysta herself had been too caught up in her own fears and doubts to pick fights with Aliyah? It had to be the anticipation of marriage soothing Aliyah's rough edges.

At that point, Chrysta suddenly realized something. Had she ever congratulated Aliyah since all of this started? From the second Greg had been introduced, all Chrysta had worried about was herself and how their parents would perceive her now that Aliyah had an edge. In all her own panic, she may have forgotten to be civil and express her pride in her sister for finding someone special. How awful and self-centered of her?

"Ally, did I ever say congrats on the engagement?" Chrysta cut through a side-discussion between Danielle and Aliyah about who knew what. Those two tended to drift off into sidebar discussions when left up to their own devices.

Aliyah rubbed her jaw absently. "I don't think you did. Or if you did, I forgot." Her shoulders jerked as she giggled. "Thank you. I appreciate the kind words." She formed a heart with her fingers and kissed mid-air with her eyes closed.

"Shame on you, Chrys, for only saying congrats now," Danielle teased as she wagged her finger. She sucked off the salt speckled on its surface. She'd apparently finished her massive bag of chips. "And here I thought the rivalry would have ended once you two got older. I guess some things never change, but that's fine." She squashed the bag between her palms. "The more you two are at each other's throats, the more people never realize what I'm up to. It's why I got away with murder while the two of you kept Mom and Dad busy in the past."

Chrysta breathed in sharply. "What? You say that like I was a problem child, too."

"Technically, you were since you would always nag me, but tonight isn't about looking back on the bad times," said Aliyah. She clasped her hands with a tender smile. "Chrysta, I don't mind the late congrats. I know you have a lot going on."

"Yes. Including the most adorable secret relationship you've kept hidden from literally everyone for months," Danielle climbed to her feet and tossed her bag in the bin near the door. She came back and sat on her mattress again. "It blows my mind to this day. Terrence is *so* cute."

All Chrysta could do was nervously laugh as they gushed over her fake fiancé. What would happen if she came clean now? Would they hate her? It was just them right now in an intimate setting. At sleepovers, people's deepest secrets always came out. It was a chance for girls to bond over what they hid from society, to strip down the perfect outer-layers of their personas.

In addition, there was the fact that her feelings for Terrence were more than fake. They were becoming genuine. She wouldn't worry so much about what her sisters would think if she could just come clean to Terrence and tell him how she felt.

But if he didn't feel the same way…

It was a fate too embarrassing to even consider.

Her lip became a chew-toy as Chrysta contemplated her next move. Perhaps now wasn't the time. Aliyah was getting married tomorrow. If she unveiled this now, it may distract from the wedding. Plus, Chrysta had done all this for that specific event. In the days leading up to it, she'd put so much effort into selling her and Terrence that sometimes, even Chrysta herself got fooled. Like at Terrence's house not too long ago.

She admired her reflection in the band of her ring. He'd seemed so sincere when he'd given it to her. Chrysta couldn't name a truer experience. Sensing the perfect fit of his mother's ring on her finger now was the icing on the cake. It had to signify something. Terrence was sweet and romantic even behind closed doors. She'd find herself wondering about what he was up to often. She gave it her all to not fall victim to his charms, but it seemed to have already happened. Why did he insist on being so perfect? Had he… caught feelings, too?

"Thanks, guys, but none of this is about me and Terrence."

Chrysta cut short her sisters' praises. "I think I'll call it a night. Tomorrow's a big day." She slipped beneath her sheets and said good night as her sisters did what they did best and made the wrong choice to stay up chitchatting. "Terrence," she whispered into her pillow. The way she felt about him was almost overwhelming. Somehow, her feelings about Terrence had gone from amicable but fake to entirely genuine. How had they become real?

More importantly, what was she going to do about it?

The morning of the wedding seemed considerably bright even before 6 a.m.

It could have been the anticipation of a union filling Terrence with hope and optimism, but whatever it was, it propelled him to drive with zeal to Chrysta's childhood home. The biggest event of Aliyah's life would commence in the afternoon, but loads of preparation was still necessary to get to that point. Yes, there were florists and other event organizers hired to assist, but only through their combined efforts and a little extra could something so major be successful.

He hadn't exactly been urged to offer his assistance with preparations, but Chrysta's mention of what had to be done gave Terrence a gist of what they were up against. Last night, he'd texted her asking if she'd appreciate his presence and help, and she'd replied with a yes. Hence his current position.

His rear-view mirror displayed clearly the freshness of his haircut. Terrence had gotten it trimmed yesterday after sleeping off the beers he'd had at Greg's. He'd been in touch with Chrysta and was happy to know she'd gotten rest, too. All attendees of the bride and groom's major parties had gotten time to recuperate. He'd found this out from both Chrysta and Greg's recent messages. Being so heavily included in their lives had come so suddenly, but boy, he was grateful for it.

He looked past his hair at the packaged suit resting on his back-seat. Hopefully, it would appear as debonair on him at the wedding as it did when he'd tried it on. This wasn't just Aliyah's big day; it was his, too. It seemed he'd managed to win over Chrysta's immediate family, but later, he'd be challenged with impressing the rest. Chrysta had stressed the importance of this via text last night, and he didn't plan on disappointing her. It still amazed him how quickly she'd bounced back from what she described as the worst hangover of her life. The memory loss didn't surprise him, though. Just as he'd anticipated, she recalled none of her drunken blabbering to him.

His mission was to win over her family first. Then, he'd win her over. He knew how she felt now, thanks to her vodka soda spree.

Now, he just had to convince her that it was okay to feel it when she was sober as well.

As Terrence cruised down the empty streets of Sweetgum, he found himself smiling. Those few seconds of heart-to-heart discussion would forever live in his mind. She may not have known it, but Terrence really had meant what he'd said. His prayer was that she'd truly appreciate the moment he formally asked. All he desired was her life shared with his. He'd been thoroughly convinced of what he wanted these past few weeks.

After killing the engine and skipping out of his vehicle, Terrence pressed the lock button on his key. He stepped onto Chrysta's parent's lawn and swallowed the crisp morning air. The sun was on its way to rising, and birds were up and about. He took some time to admire the neat neighborhood that Chrysta grew up in before his session was interrupted.

"There you are."

Terrence pocked his car keys and faced Chrysta's father. "Sir." The man's slack shorts and vest made Terrence feel right at home. He noticed the front door ajar behind him, where hired professionals ran back and forth. "And here I thought I was early. You guys seem to have been at it for hours." He walked up to the older man.

"Ha. Not me. It's the girls who've been up since who knows when micromanaging everything. I was only dragged into this about half an hour ago." The bald man slapped Terrence fondly on the arm and shook his hand.

Terrence gave a firm shake as he laughed. He overheard Aliyah crying out orders in the kitchen and made a yikes face. "Is she okay? I hope they're not ruining her vision in there. It is *her* big day. What she says goes."

The father put his hands on his hips. "Don't worry. That's just her panic slipping through. Everyone's doing as she says, but I think it's all setting in for her, so everything she says comes off like that." He held up his arms while shrugging. "That's at least what her mom and sisters have been saying."

Terrence walked with him to the door. Slowly but surely, the sun crept out of its hiding place behind the pale blue clouds. Rising early wasn't a problem for him since he did so to commute every morning, but Terrence still anticipated being groggy at this hour. Somehow, he wasn't. "Ah, I see. Their analysis makes a lot of sense." He stepped into the front door and found himself in the kitchen where the action took place. "Happy almost wedding day everyone."

Chrysta's mother was on the phone with someone while two people in black pumped balloons with helium in the adjoining living room. Aliyah seemed on her way through the side door with a stack of silver chairs, while Chrysta and Danielle were nowhere to be found. He heard chattering outside and assumed it was them. A man's voice was also audible. Greg had to be here to oversee preparations as well.

"Terrence," whispered Chrysta's mother with her phone to her chest. She waved pleasantly and then pointed to the side door. "Help the girls in the backyard." The woman returned to her phone conversation, deeply engaged in making some preparations or another.

"Yes, ma'am." Terrence bid Chrysta's dad goodbye and jogged through the open door.

His sneakers squished the damp grass as he walked under a manmade path of plastic resembling white tiles to the yard behind the house. "Looks like it's coming along already." He moved toward the aisle of similar quality and then whistled while admiring the chairs that were already here. Chrysta, Greg, and Danielle were lining up more on either side of the tiled area. So far, they still had plenty more to go.

Danielle was the first to acknowledge him. "Finally. Another pair of hands to help out." She snapped toward the bordering hedge behind the unfinished alter. It was just a single white rising. "Start organizing the other side. I know it's still early, but time flies by ultra-fast on days like these." She snuck a peep at her silver watch. Apart from that stunning piece of jewelry, Danielle's outfit this morning was on the simpler side. She wore a gray track suit and satin red bonnet. He could infer that her hair was well-done beneath the cap.

"On it." Terrence winked at Chrysta, who had just dusted her hands after placing down a chair.

Her eyes dazzled before she left her place to head toward him. Greg and Danielle continued working diligently. "Terrence, you're one in a million." Chrysta's sweats were black, and her jacket was open. It revealed a gray tank top that hugged her breasts. "I still can't believe how willing you are to lend a hand." The look in her eye said she greatly adored him for doing so.

He'd learned a thing or two about reading Chrysta since meeting her. She wasn't one to state her true feelings... except when drunk. "What did I say when you said that the first time?" Terrence smiled at her fond eye-roll. "I want to." He spoke close to her face, then held her shoulders. "So, I'm here."

Chrysta swayed like a shy school girl, then breathed out. "Thank you."

"Less talking, more working. If Aliyah comes out here and sees us slacking off, she's definitely going to have a conniption," Danielle had somehow appeared behind the alter to retrieve a few chairs. She carried them to the other side of the aisle and dropped them arbitrarily. "Chop, chop people. Chrysta, I expected better from you." She put her hands on her hips and shook her head. "Now you've got me acting like the family stick-in-the-mud."

Chrysta scoffed and shoved Danielle lightly. "Don't say that. I am *not* a stick-in-the-mud by any means." She faced Terrence. "She's lying."

"Yeah, Danielle, don't embarrass your sister in front of her fiancé." Greg carried two chairs in either arm as he carried them from the hedge to the very back part of his side of the aisle. "Though the T-man would know his girl better than anyone." He set them down in a straight line after grunting. "What do you say, Terrence? Is your girl a buzzkill?"

Terrence shook his head rapidly as Greg had a good laugh. What kind of question was that? "Absolutely not. What would you say if I asked the same about Aliyah?" He decided to get to work while they talked.

Greg cracked his back. He had on band merch. His T-shirt showcased the logo of a rock ensemble Terrence had listened to as a teen. He was tempted to ask where the man had gotten it. "There you have it, Danielle. Chrysta's A-OK." He walked to the center of the aisle and scanned it with his eyes. "Who's responsible for spicing up these chairs again?"

"The decorators who won't be here until the sun rises properly." Chrysta dragged a few chairs at her back while Terrence followed. "I personally think we should get started on our own just to make sure everything's all set. They can take care of decorating the hedges with the blue reefs Ally ordered." She placed her chairs, which Terrence added his to.

Terrence grabbed some more and brought them at record speed.

Danielle took a seat after groaning. "Why do you always force everyone to do the most, Chrysta? It's too early to decorate. I already said that after I was done out here, I was going to take a nap." She seemed a lot wearier than she had been while ordering them around mere moments ago. Terrence didn't understand the shift. "We hired decorators for a reason. You don't know anything about… okay, never mind. You're good at everything, so you may do a better job than a professional, but I won't be around when you're going the extra mile." As she complained, Greg and Terrence kept working.

Greg put down a few more chairs and counted. He got his phone and squinted at the screen. "Still got a whole lot more to set up, but so it goes." The man hummed, seemingly unaffected by the workload. "I actually trust Chrysta with decorating. What I'm worried about is how she'll do the rest by herself. Even for Chrysta, that's a mighty task. Look at all these chairs!"

Terrence just finished the third row. "She won't be doing anything alone with me here." He wrapped his arm around the hardworking woman. "I know a thing or two about wedding decorating, so I think I'll be useful in assisting." He lived for the way she got shy by his compliments.

Chrysta giggled. "I wouldn't want it any other way." She held his arm on her shoulders. "Anyway, the first order of business is setting all these chairs up. When we're done, I'll fetch the baby blue and silver cloth to start us off." She bolted away from Terrence and went back to chair-arranging.

❦

THE SNACKS PROVIDED by Chrysta's mom had been filling. Terrence hadn't known homemade cupcakes could be so delicious. The only other person who'd ever made him drool over pastries was his own mother.

"Oh my gosh, you've gotten so much done *way* before the ceremony. That'll leave us *tons* of time to get dressed and record for my documentary!" Aliyah was a bundle of delight when she came out to oversee the progress on the backyard. During the time between when they'd started and now, the actual decorators had arrived. They were currently assembling a wedding bower behind the alter. Things were coming along.

Chrysta pointed her chin up after showing her sister the silky blue and silver cloth decorations hanging as hoops on the seats along the aisle. "What can I say? No task is too grand for Chrysta and her assistant, Terrence." She nudged Terrence in the rib.

"Don't take all the credit. Terrence did most of the heavy lifting. You mainly told him what to do." Danielle rotated her shoulder muscle before casting a glance at her watch. "Wait. Is mom almost done setting up inside for the reception?"

Terrence recalled the woman's last update on her progress. She'd complained about needing to replace the curtains and other unfinished chores after serving them treats. Come to think of it, she'd even mentioned how slow her brunch preparations were taking. He loved her maternal nature of giving but was certain she'd taken on too much. "The decorators should be helping her out with that. Wasn't your dad lending a hand?" He'd been facing the weary Danielle but looked to Chrysta on his last sentence.

She'd apparently been looking his way all along. Her deep brown eyes twinkled with intrigue at his words.

He stumbled on his statement after noticing her attention. Had anyone ever looked more gorgeous while simply listening? "Your dad…"

"Yes, he should be helping out too, but the decorators aren't here to clean up. The house is huge. We should go help with sweeping and polishing." Chrysta sounded upbeat about taking on extra work. Terrence liked her pep, but Aliyah and Danielle groaned.

"Let the men handle it. Mom shouldn't have to lift another finger with Dad, Greg, and Terrence here." Aliyah sat, and her phone appeared in milliseconds. She began taking selfies and recording herself. "Prepping for the big day. Got the hubby here and my bridesmaids. Everyone, say hey."

Terrence lifted his hand to wave, but Chrysta grabbed it. His face heated as she tugged him back to the house.

"Let's help inside before brunch. If we all pitch in, this place will be ready by 11 a.m.!" Chrysta hopped to the door like a bubbly kid, and Terrence simply followed. He'd gladly let Chrysta drag him to the underworld if she wanted to see it. All Terrence cared about now was spending extra time with her. It didn't matter what they did. As long as they were together.

They were directed to an open room attached to the living room. There were seats stacked in a corner and tables there, too. It seemed the delivery guys had brought them here for setting up later. But before that could happen, the room had to be cleaned.

Terrence picked up a broom and started sweeping the left side of the room.

Chrysta chose the right and was now sweeping with vigor. "When we're done, they're going to want to hire us for wedding preps everywhere." She panted.

Terrence was much slower but efficient regardless. "Don't put too much into working, or you may not have the energy to party. I think Aliyah would want her maid of honor to be as energetic as possible for her big ceremony and after-party." He moved closer to Chrysta the more he swept.

She inched closer to him, too. They could collide in the middle of the room if they kept up their pace. "You're right, but trust me. I won't be tired." She smiled at him between breaths. "I've always been great at taking on a lot and coming through when I'm needed. It's just who I am. Not to brag, but…"

Terrence laughed. "It's not bragging if I asked." He paused and held his broom to the side. "Would you say that deep down you can't wait for Aliyah and Greg to tie the knot so the pressure of a wedding won't be something you have to worry about anymore?"

Chrysta stopped to huff and puff. "I'd be lying if I said I wasn't." She went back to it, gathering large piles of dust in record time. "And I bet you're just itching to get back to your normal little tailor life where you don't have to act like you're in love with a stranger."

Terrence had forgotten they'd never made anything official. Chrysta had no clue what he was planning. She'd been out of sorts when he confessed. "If I'm being honest..." He stared at the wooden floor. Scattered dust particles formed a short path where he'd swept them. "Getting involved with all this was some of the most fun I've had in ages. You, your family, and everyone else have been so kind. Getting to know you was honestly a blessing." He knew she felt the same. Her drunken brain had already told him.

Chrysta looked as if 'melted' was a person. Her eyes were liquid, and her lip trembled with the emotions she was trying to hold back. "Come here." She dropped her broom and went in for a hug.

Terrence held her so tight she squealed. "Oh, sorry. Too much?" He'd been ready to lift her off the ground.

At that instance, she did the most endearing thing he could fathom and rested her chin on his chest to look at him. "No. I like bear hugs."

They shared a brief laugh before getting back to work.

The two finished sweeping just in time for brunch. They'd covered the entire bottom floor in just an hour; the house was pretty huge. Luckily, upstairs was off-limits, so there was no need to clean it. Apparently, Chrysta's dad had vacuumed earlier, but that was all.

"Here you go, Terrence. For the gentle man who's always willing to help." Chrysta's mom handed him a plate with a burger on it. Aliyah, Greg, and Danielle had found places to eat around the kitchen. Terrence noticed Chrysta heading to the living room and caught up once he'd thanked her mother. As he sat beside Chrysta, he found more decorators entering to adorn the lovely home. If he'd grown up in a place like this, he would get married here too.

"Your mom has an eye for aesthetics. She managed to make both her cupcakes and burgers look like the food in million-dollar commercials. " He rested his paper plate on the short table in front of him.

Chrysta had cut her burger into four neat triangles. She held one, and doing so allowed him a full view of her stellar nails. They were painted a soft shade of blue with speckled rhinestones. "I know. I guess you can say it's where I get it from. Or maybe that her food is what I keep in mind whenever I make something. Everything *has* to look and *taste* fantastic." She fit the triangle in her mouth.

Terrence took a massive bite out of his. As burger juice soaked his tongue with flavor, several emotions hit him at once. Here he was, sitting beside one of the most beautiful women he'd ever met. Her welcoming family laughed and ate in content in the next room while hired professionals added the finishing touches to their home in preparation for a life-changing ceremony. One that he got to be part of because Chrysta happened to need a date. Both her parents spoke to him like their own, and her sister's fiancé treated him like a brother. It wasn't that Terrence was a loner in any way, but after his dad passed some years ago, he'd been missing something. To feel a sense of belonging within a family was a gift he'd taken for granted growing up. Terrence hadn't even noticed he'd lost that until now when he finally felt it again.

"I like that she puts her all into whatever she does. I can also taste the love, too," he stated once he'd swallowed what he bit. "It's great." How could he let Chrysta know how much he enjoyed just sitting here without coming off as sappy?

Chrysta pinched another burger triangle between her eye-catching fingers with their marvelous nails. "She'd love to hear you say that. Make sure you tell her before we all start getting ready." She peeped into the kitchen. "Looks like we don't have much time. I'm just glad we managed to get everything done before the afternoon. The wedding's at three, so I think we've given ourselves more than enough time to get ready." She munched down on her burger. "Although knowing Ally, she'll definitely need more than three hours to get dressed. Especially for a day like today. Even if her hair and nails are already done."

"I can't blame her. Let's just hope the guests won't be mad if we're a little late."

"It's not about the guests but Ally herself. She wants the sun to set when she says her vows. If we're off schedule, then that won't happen." Chrysta blew a raspberry and dusted her hands off. "I can see the tantrum now."

Terrence shook his head. "I'm sure we'll be on time. Look, she's already packing up to start going upstairs." He, too, was staring into the kitchen. Aliyah had just thrown her paper plate away to run to the stairs. There was something like panic on her face as she zipped off. "Is she okay?"

Chrysta turned on the couch when Aliyah placed her foot on the first step. "What's going on? Are you going up to get ready, or did something happen?"

Aliyah paused with her hand on the railing. "My makeup girl is stuck in traffic, so she'll be here later than anticipated! Talk about bad luck on your wedding day." She screamed softly, then ran up with flailing arms. "I'm going to hop in the shower! Everyone else, start putting orders to yourselves! It's go-time!" Some of that got lost when she reached the upper floor, but the sentiment was felt.

Chrysta stuffed the rest of her food into her mouth as Greg and Danielle strolled after the hyper Aliyah.

"She said she's on her way, and traffic is minimal. Why are you panicking?" Greg groaned, then jogged up the stairs with Danielle, who laughed.

"What a Bridezilla!" Danielle skipped behind Greg until she was out of their sight as well.

Terrence and Chrysta sat silently for a second, then looked at each other.

"What just happened?" Terrence asked with a laugh.

"Sounds like Aliyah misunderstood something, but that's

normal." Chrysta finished her food. "Aliyah can be a lot to begin with, and today, even more than usual."

"Ah, I see," Terrence replied.

Chrysta dusted off her fingers. "Okay. We need to get ready regardless of whether she'd been overreacting or not. Come on. Eat up so you can toss that plate in the trash." She was on her feet and clapping in Terrence's face. "You brought your suit with you to change here, right?"

"Of course I did," Terrence said with a full mouth. He apologized for his lack of manners, then chewed faster. Once everything went down his esophagus, he spoke again. The decorators were on their way here, which meant they *had* to get a move on. "I'll go get it now."

"Awesome. Let me throw these out." Chrysta took his empty plate and crushed it along with hers.

Just watching her fold them both till they fit between her hands as a small ball moved him enough to speak up. "Can I just... say something?"

"What is it?" Chrysta batted her naturally lengthy lashes. They were like butterfly wings flapping in a summer breeze.

Terrence didn't want to hold things up, but if he held it in any longer, he may never get the chance. "Being with your family this morning has been a lot of fun. I know we've been busy and running around like scrambling mice, but somehow, getting work done with people you know you belong with is ten times more fulfilling than doing so alone. I... I've really felt like part of the family these past few days. I didn't realize that was something I'd been missing until you welcomed me into your home, and everyone opened their arms. So, thanks. Just in case I don't get to say it before things start going crazy. I can already hear Aliyah squealing upstairs." He aimed a finger at the upper floor where stomping feet were very much audible.

Chrysta's mom ran to the stairs. "Aliyah, your makeup artist just rolled up in front of the house. Stop throwing a tantrum!" She marched back to the kitchen, muttering about all Aliyah's theatrics.

Terrence heard Chrysta's dad coming in through the front door laughing. The man said something along the lines of 'this is expected' before walking Aliyah's makeup artist to the stairs. The man then found himself in the kitchen to assist Chrysta's mom with clearing the counters and table.

Chrysta seemed surprised that Terrence would say that. "Terrence, you are *absolutely* welcome." Her blinking eyes and stuttering led him to think he'd stolen her words. "I didn't expect you to thank me for something like that. Have you been... a little lonely after everything with your parents?" She stepped closer, her voice growing softer.

He scratched his head at memories of family dinners that hadn't happened since he was a teen. His father's smile at their dining room table returned as a distant thought before images of Chrysta's dad patting his back and her family sharing stories resurfaced. He thought of their banter outside while setting up and his time spent with Greg's friends a few days ago. When all of these took over Terrence's headspace, an emotion he had not taken note of disappeared to be replaced by joy. Perhaps that feeling *had* been loneliness. Chrysta hit the nail exactly. "I guess so. But now it's gone, and I'm just happy I've gotten to spend so much time with everyone in your family. Especially you."

She once again seemed lost for words. Chrysta lowered her face while wearing a tiny smile, then squeezed his shoulder. "I know. You never hesitate to let me know you've enjoyed what we have... whatever it is." She turned her face and gave him her cheek.

What did that mean? Was the onus on him to name what they were? Should he do so now?

Terrence fought his doubts to speak up. Should he ask what Chrysta wanted to call them or say at this instance that they were together? What was the best call, and was now the time to decide?

Why was he suddenly frozen? He'd been so confident over the phone. "Chrysta, I really want us—"

Rushed, heavy footsteps pounded the carpeted stairs before they abruptly stopped. They both turned when the last step was stomped on and saw Aliyah at the end of the stairs. "Why are you love birds standing around looking all doe-eyed? We have a wedding later, and no one here is going to make me late!" Her face was in the beginning stages of makeup application. "Chrys, hurry! Stop distracting Terrence!"

"I'm not! I'm not!" Chrysta rolled her eyes and ran to the kitchen. "Get your suit, Terrence!" She ran past the angered Aliyah on her way. "And you, head upstairs! You look ridiculous. Don't waste your own time."

Aliyah zoomed back up after arguing briefly with Chrysta.

Terrence couldn't believe how that ended. *Next time.* He'd at least gotten to thank her for her incredible family. "Next time."

CHAPTER SEVENTEEN

"Not long now."

Chrysta sealed her lipstick and puckered her peach lips. According to the mirror on her dresser, the color went perfectly with her dress. She'd been scared that none of her makeup would go with it.

The woman got up and reversed from the mirror. She straightened her dress while expelling air from her mouth. "This is it." Why was her heart pounding like a sledgehammer when today wasn't hers? So far, everything from the banter with her family to Terrence's heartfelt words had set the day up to be great. Optimistic guests were filling the backyard as she spoke. Somehow, Chrysta could hear the buzz of their conversations even this far from the action. The gorgeous decorations, her fellow bridesmaids jumping off the walls in the rooms around hers, and the heavenly symphonies traveling from the altar should have made a positive impact on her mood, but somehow, it all felt off.

Right as Chrysta squeezed her phony engagement ring, two knocks at her door snapped her out of the trance she'd fallen into. "Danielle."

Danielle was a vision this afternoon. Her silver heels clunked against the carpet as she stepped inside Chrysta's room. From the shiny coils of black hanging from her scalp to the luscious lashes batting when she blinked, all added to the art of her look. "Oh my gosh, you look *amazing,* Chrysta. You're like a princess." She opened her arms with a pouting lip.

Chrysta flipped her own hanging curls to accept her sister's embrace. As they held on dearly, her reality set in. One of *her* little sisters would be married on the compound they grew up on in just a few hours. Where had the time gone, and what had she done with it? What was this sense of lack? How could she be both proud and empty on such an occasion? "Thank you, honey. You look gorgeous, too. The hair, makeup, and shoes… it's all so fabulous I could cry." She heard heels hitting the halls and rooms outside. "Is Aliyah ready? What about the guys? Greg?" Greg's groomsmen had arrived an hour ago to dress here, too.

"You know men. They've been dressed for thirty minutes. I heard them moving down to the altar. *We're* the ones who are late." Danielle put her arm around Chrysta's waist while holding up her phone. "We need to capture every second of beauty for our sister's big day." She smiled brightly while snapping a picture.

Chrysta had posed just in time. She noticed their mom appearing in the doorway after Danielle held her phone down. "Aww, Mom. You look great." She walked carefully to the older woman in red. It certainly was the lady's color. Her nails and lips matched perfectly.

"Thank you, sweetheart." Their mom looked antsy but happy all at once. Chrysta's supposed nerves were natural on such a big day. "You girls are ready, so follow me. I need to address all of you before we get this show on the road." She chewed gum between the words of her sentence.

"Where are we going?" Chrysta asked as she and Danielle entered the hall with their mother. She heard talking from Danielle's room across the hall and saw Greg's sister on the phone. Her dress fit perfectly and complimented every curve on her body.

"Aliyah's room, of course." The mother walked them right to the locked door, down the hall, and knocked. "When I last peeped in, she'd been getting her lipstick applied. I'm sure that she's ready now." She smiled at Chrysta before knocking on the door, hiding her cell phone behind the pleats of her dress.

They were allowed in by Aliyah's makeup artist. Another woman was here taking photos of Aliyah by the window. Just like Danielle, Aliyah was the perfect picture of beauty. Her Cinderella wedding dress twinkled with silver studs in the upper region. Aliyah's black hair was pinned up in a gorgeous bun decorated with white dove clips. If fantasies could come to life, they'd look like Aliyah in her wedding dress.

"Hi, guys," she said after the last flash shone. She was assisted to the area next to her bed by the photographer. "Everyone looks so great. This is insane." Her words were on-brand, but her face didn't at all match her enthusiasm.

Chrysta eyed the way her sister rubbed her stomach and took deep breaths sporadically. "Your dress, makeup, and heels are beautiful too. Look at you." Aliyah's partial smile at the remark ticked Chrysta off. "Are you…"

"Okay, girls, you can compliment each other later." Their mom found herself in front of them.

Aliyah said goodbye to her makeup artist and photographer before fanning her face and exhaling quietly. "What is it, Mom? Any second now, Dad will be coming through those doors to say that they're ready." She seemed more relaxed, but the discomfort was still evident.

At least to Chrysta, it was. She could have been projecting since her own sense of dread was still very much apparent.

"I know, I know, but…" The pride in their mother's eyes was somehow bittersweet to watch. The woman held her phone to her face. "I'd just like to share this with all of you before Ally's big moment. You know…" She smiled with glossy eyes. "Every mother dreams of seeing her little girls grow into beautiful, bold, and independent women, and I can safely say that I've witnessed this with all of you."

Chrysta gulped as their mom began to recite something from her phone screen. Independent. That word lingered. Could Chrysta call herself that after the lengths she'd gone to just to please the very woman who deemed her as such? Anyone possessing a shred of independence would have enough self-worth to not lie for the sole sake of gaining someone's approval.

"All birds must leave the nest. Even when they're unsure what comes next. Mommy has held your hand for long enough. But now it's time that you show the world that you're tough. With what I've given you, please live life to the fullest. And make your own lives the most wonderful." Their mom lowered her phone with a nod. "I'm proud of all of you and so, so happy that Ally is on track to building her own life. Chrysta's turn will come soon, but for now, this is Ally's big day. Again, I am just overwhelmed by how you each turned out. Living your own lives and shaping them how you want them to be. It's been the greatest gift to raise you."

Chrysta didn't know what to say. The emptiness returned with a vengeance as Danielle bombarded their mom with a tight hug. Aliyah was next, and soon, a three-way hug was in order. Chrysta would join them, but... their mom's words hurt. She'd centered her life around pleasing her parents for so long. It wasn't just an issue from childhood, either. She'd carried it into adulthood and would probably keep living how she believed they wanted her to if something didn't change.

But where had this attitude stemmed from? A lack of validation growing up? Or was Chrysta just a people-pleaser? No one was born itching to satisfy others. But, still, she couldn't stop herself. Her parents loved her deeply, and she loved them as well. Sometimes, just wanting to do right by the people that you loved made you want to please them as well.

There was nothing wrong with doing things that made the people you loved happy.

However, Chrysta was beginning to think that it was happening at the expense of things that she wanted as well.

And that, more than anything, did seem like a problem.

"Chryssie, join in," her mom requested, with Danielle and Aliyah on either arm.

Chrysta swallowed her sulks to smile. "Sure." These issues would be dealt with later. She'd one day confront her parents on the matter, but not during Aliyah's moment. It was just good to know that she'd realized what the problem had been all these years. From now on, she'd work to change her mindset.

Their mother pecked them each with a kiss. She let go before swiping the bottom of her eyes as if tears had fallen from them. "Is my mascara running?"

Chrysta smiled painfully as Danielle helped their mom by fanning her face. Aliyah seemed ready to add to the hysterics. "Calm down, everyone." Chrysta did what she did best and brought order to the scene. The room was suddenly much wider. Life itself felt far and out of reach. Was Chrysta having some sort of quiet crisis? "Mom, you're not crying, but I can tell you're emotional, and Aliyah…"

Her normally bold and confident younger sister looked at her nervously.

Chrysta wondered if the pressure of the biggest event of her life was only now setting in. "You need to breathe before you go out there." She heard footsteps down the hall through the door. They'd left it partially open. "If you don't calm down and take it all in slowly, you might end up falling apart on the altar."

"Wow. Way to ease the pressure, Chrys." Danielle was rubbing their mother's back. "I think Mom's heartfelt poem just got to her. She's all right."

Aliyah touched her belly while inhaling through her lips. "Yes. I'm completely fine."

Chrysta wished she could say the same. "Great. And thanks, Mom, for everything." She couldn't look the woman in the eye while speaking. Her mom seemed to notice but didn't utter a word since their father flung the door open in a flash.

"It's showtime." He folded his hands in the doorway while chuckling. "Okay, girls. We said the wedding would be at three and my watch says it's about that hour. We wouldn't want to miss the setting sun because we lingered inside too long now, would we? It's time to let your old man hold your hand and hand you over to the man of your dreams." The man held his arm out after fixing his tie.

Aliyah looked unsure as to whether to hold their dad or not. She looked from their mother to Chrysta and, for some reason, stayed on Chrysta.

Throughout their childhood, Aliyah never cared much for Chrysta's word on anything. It was actually more likely that she'd go directly against Chrysta's advice. It felt strange seeing her await Chrysta's permission.

Chrysta nodded, and Aliyah did so, too. The younger woman now clutched onto their father dearly. She seemed calmer but also on edge. Chrysta would at least expect some semblance of excitement. Was there something Aliyah was hiding? Why did she seem so… guilt-ridden?

Just as they followed Aliyah and their dad into the hallway, someone came running up to them.

Chrysta had thought that all the guests were waiting down in the yard. Why was Terrence here with that look on his face? "Everything okay?" When he stopped jogging, they paused too.

Terrence aimed a thumb over his shoulder. "There's been a bit of a development."

Silence.

As everyone's mouths remained glued shut, Chrysta took it upon herself to question this. "What development? What do you mean?" She stepped to Aliyah's side as the bride gaped at Terrence.

Terrence scratched his head. "Greg told everyone that the wedding would start shortly before leaving the altar. We'd all expected he'd come back by now, but no one's seen him. His groom's men have been trying to call him, but he's not picking up." He opened his arms. "I hate to be the bearer of bad news, but something's definitely up, and whatever it is isn't good."

"Oh my God." Their mom covered her mouth and walked slowly in the other direction.

"Terrence, what are you saying? Are you sure he's not just planning a surprise?" Danielle went from shocked to accusatory. She seemed ready to grab Terrence's collar.

"Calm down, calm down." Their dad went to check on their mom while Terrence rushed out more justifications for his assumptions.

"He said so fifteen minutes ago, and like I said, his friends can't reach him. I'm sorry." Terrence stepped away as Danielle proceeded to lash out.

Chrysta instinctively dragged Danielle back and commanded her to relax. She then turned to Aliyah, who was one shade lighter from seeming ghostly. "Ally? Everything okay? You... you heard what Terrence just said, right? That... Greg...."

It was then that everyone stopped their over-the-top reactions to check on the bride, who hadn't said a thing since Terrence broke the unfortunate news.

Aliyah's eyes were stuck wide open. She finally unstuck them from where they'd been glued to the floor to turn to Chrysta.

Chrysta gulped. "Al—"

Aliyah threw up.

CHAPTER EIGHTEEN

In his field of work, Terrence had heard dozens of horror stories involving grooms getting cold feet and ruining what was meant to be the most beautiful day of a woman's life. They usually came with refund requests on purchased dresses. He'd always just shake his head when the stories were shared at the shop, but being here to witness one first-hand was *nothing* like overhearing an account.

This was awful. Full-on, terribly, awful.

"Breathe, Aliyah, you need to breathe. *Breathe* in and out, or the next thing you know, you'll be passed out on the carpet." Chrysta held Aliyah's hand as the traumatized bride leaned against the wall and cried her eyes out. Barf still soaked the carpet, but no one had made a move to clean it. Terrence considered Aliyah lucky not to have ruined her custom-made dress.

"He left me! He left me before we could even say 'I do'! I should have known this would happen. They always lose interest when they find out!" Aliyah was a wailing, blubbering mess of tears and despair. She slid to the floor and sat on her bum, holding her face and falling apart.

Terrence stepped back as the women of the family squatted and stooped to console her. Her father just held his face and shook his head in what Terrence presumed was stifled anger. Terrence honestly wasn't sure where he fit in all of this. It seemed like more of an issue for the family. Aliyah may probably prefer to be alone right now. Or at least away from anyone she wasn't related to. "I think I'll leave now." His phone got a message then, and he opened it. "Okay, it seems like the groom's men and Greg's family are searching the property for him." Considering how large the yard and house were, it may be a while until they found him. Terrence hadn't known that estates in Sweetgum existed, if Chrysta's family property could even be considered one. It just seemed too large for 'house' to be adequate.

"Do they really think he's still here? He probably drove off to hide in a corner or something. You know how these grooms can be. Boy, do I hate cowards." Danielle was on her knees beside the bawling Aliyah. She rubbed her arm and handed her tissues. "It's okay. This isn't your fault. It isn't your fault."

Aliyah seemed averse to any of their comforts. "No, but it *is* my fault!" She held her stomach with her hands. "It always happens this way." She looked up at Terrence.

Terrence found her tear-filled eyes difficult to make contact with. "What do you mean?" He really shouldn't be here. Why was Aliyah pulling him in by directing questions at him? Now the family was staring. Danielle seemed ready to bite his neck while Chrysta bit her lip in clear discomfort.

Aliyah sniffed, then dipped her chin to her chest.

"Ally, what are you talking about? We won't know unless you tell us." Chrysta got down on her knees in front of her.

Aliyah grabbed her forehead with both hands and groaned to the ceiling. "I'm pregnant."

Terrence blinked in stun. He heard gasps from Danielle and their mom before several questions followed. "Pregnant." The gears in his brain began to turn. A rushed wedding with a man who Chrysta said 'popped out of nowhere,' Aliyah's emotions throughout the planning phases… this whole wedding had to have been orchestrated due to the pregnancy. He couldn't say for sure, but it did seem that way from his end.

"He could have just said he didn't want me or our baby. Why'd he let it get this far? Why did he wait to leave me at the altar like this? Pregnancies always scare them off. I don't even know *how* he let it get this far!" Aliyah wouldn't stop blubbering on the floor.

Chrysta rubbed her shoulder and wiped the tears from her eyes. "Okay, okay. I know that you're going through a lot of emotions, but there's probably still hope."

"Hope?" Their dad's fists were clenched at his sides, and the creases on his forehead were more intense than before. "Any man who leaves a woman like that doesn't deserve a second chance."

Their mother shook her head. "Honey, please." She held his arm as he went on to chastise Greg. "We don't know what happened. For all we know, he could have hit his head somewhere on this property. He did say that the wedding would proceed shortly. He might be hurt." Her maternal nature shone in these words.

"That was all talk. He ran off. Did you see his car parked outside on your way here, Terrence?" Danielle climbed to her feet while Chrysta gently helped Aliyah. "He had to have driven away."

Terrence still felt out of place. He gave Danielle's question some thought before nodding. "Yes. His car is still parked on the property, so I'm sure he's around here somewhere." He scratched his arm. "I think I better go—"

"Before you do," said Chrysta. Aliyah's limp arm was hanging off her shoulder. The disheveled bride seemed unwilling to walk on her own. Her pained sobs nearly drowned out what Chrysta said next. "Can you do me a favor and make Aliyah some tea? I think she needs a soother." She seemed to feel guilty for asking.

"Of course." Terrence didn't mind assisting from a distance. Once he handed over that tea, he'd be off. With an extra pair of hands on board the Greg search team, Terrence bet they'd locate him soon.

HE'D LEFT the warm cup of ginger spice tea in Chrysta's hands a minute ago. They'd taken Aliyah into her room, where she'd been stretched out across her bed. Terrence wasn't sure if she'd drink what he made her, but he'd leave that task up to Chrysta and the rest of the family. His job now was finding Greg.

"Any sign of him?" he asked after walking down the aisle. Devon was the sole groom's man remaining at the altar. The others had scattered in hopes of pinpointing Greg's hiding place.

Devon just dropped his phone into his back pocket. "Nope. I went around asking neighbors if they'd spotted him and got nothing. The other guys have checked the garage, the rooms, the old dog house, and even the treehouse." He sighed with a shake of his head. "The guests are getting restless."

Terrence could see a few of them going live on social media. This had to be the textbook definition of humiliating. Why would Greg take off like this? He hadn't struck Terrence as the type to abandon his bride at the bachelor party. He'd seemed all about Aliyah and their budding relationship. But Terrence supposed that someone who'd up and run off on their wedding day would never reveal they were capable of such. "So basically... they've checked *everywhere* and haven't found him."

Devon scratched the stubble on his chin. His beard was well-shaped for the occasion. "I mean, around the west wing of the house has got this broken old tool shed that no one could open. I tried getting in, but the door was too swollen. I don't think anyone's capable of getting in or out of that thing. Plus, we checked through the windows and saw nothing but tools all over the place. There's no way he's hiding in there." He held the side of his head before shaking it. "This is *so* not like Greg though. He's a straight-up man. It's almost like he's lost his mind or something." He sat on the short flight of stairs leading up to the altar. "I'm starting to think he went to go pick something up and hurt himself. The guy has got to be knocked out. I refuse to believe that such an honest and cool guy would leave his wedding prematurely like this." He rubbed his palm against his fade. "I don't know what to do."

Terrence digested these words before marching to the back of the altar. He circled around the small pond nearby. It reflected the dim sky.

"Where are you going?" Devon asked.

Terrence told him to give him a minute before running to the west wing from the back of the house. The ancient treehouse stared down at him on his way. He ignored the fact that his shiny leather shoes got mud on them from the damp grass watered by sprinklers and kept walking.

As Terrence walked alongside the west wall, he used his eyes to scan the area Devon had spoken of. There was no one here. He saw the other groomsmen congregated around the front yard with phones out after making it to the front, but there was no sign of Greg. Terrence reversed before making a beeline for the supposed unbreakable shed beside the house. He kicked on the swollen wooden door. The short wooden structure rattled under his mighty kick, but Terrence persisted.

Metal items clanged and clattered inside as he gave his everything to kick the door in. Greg *had* to be in there. Terrence wasn't sure how he'd entered, but where else could he have gone if his car was parked there and no neighbors had witnessed him taking off?

"Open already!" Terrence delivered a final kick, which caused his foot to break a hole in the door. "Ah!" He winced at the shock of his action and then dragged his foot out. Had he actually done that?

The man fit his hand through the hole and felt for a doorknob. It may be no use turning it, but he was becoming kind of desperate. Aliyah at least deserved an explanation. Chrysta did, too. She'd done so much to prepare for this day. Plus, there was also the possibility that Greg had somehow wandered in here and gotten hurt. Terrence just wanted some answers.

"The back door."

Terrence froze at the voice that spoke from inside. He dragged his arm out and stepped back. Was he hearing things?

"There's a back door. Once you get past the hedge, it's not hard to get through." The lackluster voice dragged on.

Terrence's mouth remained open before he ran around the shed to follow these instructions.

Lo and behold, there truly was a backdoor almost swallowed by the property's surrounding hedge. He squeezed himself between the prickly twigs and wooden door, then reached for the knob. Terrence would have never known it was here without being told. He twisted the rusty door handle and pushed himself inside.

Terrence panted in the face of a stoic Greg standing before a wooden wall. There were shovels and spades hanging to his left and bags of old fertilizer opened on the ground. This seemed like some sort of secret compartment designated for gardening supplies. Had Greg been hiding here this entire time? No wonder the guys hadn't spotted him through the window.

"Greg." Terrence wiped sweat from his face and cringed at the state of his own suit. It was a mess of cobwebs, and there were rips in the leg of his dress pants. "*What* are you doing here?" It was now clear as day to Terrence that Greg hadn't fallen victim to some tragic accident.

Greg said nothing for far too long. He walked over to a short bench under the gardening tools hanging on the wall and sat there. The man twiddled his thumbs with an uncertain stare, pointing to the ground.

Terrence's first inclination was to chastise the man for abandoning his bride, but he took another approach. "Greg." He sat beside him and faced Greg silently. The other man's pensive expression filled Terrence with even more questions than he'd initially had. "We all know Aliyah's pregnant."

That got Greg to stop looking elsewhere. He faced Terrence with widened eyes before shaking his head. "So, she told everyone." The man rubbed his palms against the black pants of his suit. "How is she?"

Terrence wondered what this meant. "Awful. She's crying, she threw up, and last I heard, she said that you were leaving her and your baby." He frowned. "Greg, are you only marrying Aliyah because she's having your baby? Was that the plan all along? Have you only now realized that this may not be the best course of action?" He didn't mean to sound accusatory, but perhaps prompting Greg would get him to open up.

Greg rubbed his forehead and sat back. His weight caused the wooden wall to creak. "No." He shook his head. "I *love* Aliyah. She's crazy in the best way; she's drop-dead gorgeous, and she knows how to have fun. Ever since I've met her, she's all I've thought about."

Terrence could relate to that last part. Chrysta sure had stolen his mind since he'd laid eyes on her. He'd let her live there as long as she wanted. "Okay, so what's all this? Why are you sitting in here when you should be out on that altar?"

Greg sucked his teeth in agitation. "I don't know." He fidgeted with a shaking head.

Not the answer Terrence was hoping for. "You don't *know*?" He searched the floor for answers. "How can you not know? Greg, aren't you the one who got down on one knee?"

"I did. And I meant what I did. It's just that..." Greg tapped his thumbs together before finally facing Terrence. "My parents had a messy divorce, and I've heard that the marriage someone grew up with as a kid reflects what they'll have as an adult."

That was a first for Terrence. He saw the beautiful love shared between his mom and dad and then imagined Chrysta. If there was any truth to this, then it meant great things for him. But he couldn't let himself be sidetracked. "Who said that? You're not your parents, and neither is Aliyah. Is that really why you're in here?" That divorce must have truly been horrendous if it rendered Greg to this on his wedding day. Come to think of it, the family photos Terrence had seen at Greg's house sort of reflected this. He'd never seen both of Greg's parents in pictures with him. It was always either one or the other. Had it been so bad that they couldn't even stomach a family photo?

"You won't understand." Greg slumped forward with elbows on his lap. "It's not something I talk about, but before they divorced, they were constantly at each other's throats, and after it happened, I wasn't even allowed to mention one in front of the other. I'd always vowed that when I got married, we'd stay together and never become that toxic, but now I'm not sure. Life is messy, Terrence. What if something happens, and Aliyah and I become exactly like them? What if we traumatize our kid? Then, I'll become my own worst nightmare. I can't… wouldn't it be better for us to never have been together so our child will never have to witness something so horrible? We can be cordial and friendly around them as separate people. If we get married, it may complicate things."

Terrence had never heard Greg so apprehensive. "Greg," he grabbed the man's shoulder. "This is your life, and you're in control of what happens in it. Your parents' time has gone. Don't let what happened with them stop you from…" He heard his own words and trailed off. Terrence had been holding off on tying the knot with anyone with the hopes of finding a love as pure as his parents'. He'd gotten over that after meeting Chrysta but still hadn't made a definite move. Was that perhaps still hindering him? He hadn't so much as asked her out. Yes, there was the possibility of Chrysta not reciprocating his feelings exactly, but Terrence would only know if she did after making it clear how he saw her. It hadn't even occurred to him that this may have been a factor affecting his pursuit for anything permanent with not only Chrysta but all potential love interests.

His lonely bachelor life could be traced back to the unrealistic standards of love set up by his folks. He'd just desired pure love so deeply that he'd forgotten to open his heart to any love at all. But luckily, despite the long, drawn-out wait he'd forced upon himself, he'd managed to stumble into something incredible. He'd met Chrysta and was now ready to kick things up a notch now that he'd detected this pattern. So maybe the eternal waiting was worth it. At least now he knew for sure who he desired.

Terrence tried again. "Don't let whatever went down with your parents stop you from doing what your heart knows is right. If you keep letting their mistakes make decisions for you, you'll never move forward." He spoke earnestly to the man staring at his lap.

Greg sat in silence with eyes that seemed to scrutinize the floor.

Terrence touched the man's shoulder. "Plus, I can say for sure that you're already on the right track to being a wholesome example for your kid because you're putting his or her emotions before your own. Your main worry seems to be that you'll be a source of trauma for your kid. Thinking along those lines makes me believe that you won't be capable of hurting them if you try. So quit pressuring yourself. It will be fine. You love Aliyah, she loves you, and all your guests are waiting, so why not just go through with everything?" He realized he may come off as pushy, so he drew back his hand. "But it's really up to you. I'm just here to assist in making a decision."

The groom massaged his knees with the palms of his hands. He seemed to think deeply before nodding. "Okay. I think you're right." He winced. "Although I'm not sure how willing Aliyah will be to marry me after this whole fiasco."

Terrence winced while picturing the frazzled bride he'd left upstairs. Was she in any state to walk down the aisle? This whole situation would tip anyone off the edge and leave them with doubts. It may be wise to ask Aliyah first before making any announcements. "I think she can probably speak for herself on that matter."

Greg barked out a sad laugh. "Yeah. Right. If she'll talk to me."

Terrence shrugged. "It can't hurt to try. Would you like to talk to her?" He fished for his phone in his pocket. "She's kind of in shambles."

Greg's gulp was loud. "Maybe doing so over the phone really is best at this stage." He got up. "Can you call her?" He scratched his head.

Terrence willingly assisted by contacting Chrysta.

"Hello? Did you find him, Terrence? Where are you? Devon just came up here looking for you. How did two men manage to get lost in one afternoon? It's almost nightfall." Chrysta whispered firmly over the phone.

Terrence could feel Greg's eyes drilling holes into his skull. The man was standing akimbo over him. "Don't worry. I haven't run off. I just happened to find Greg's hiding spot. We're both in the shed on the west wing of your property." He heard wailing and bawling on Chrysta's end. The guilt clutched his throat.

"You found him?" Chrysta's volume went up a few decibels. "That's great. What did he say? What's going on? Is the wedding really off? Is he okay?"

Terrence eyed the now nervously pacing Greg. "He's all right. He'd just been worried about his and Aliyah's marriage going south because of the sour marriage his parents had." He saw Greg wiping his hands against the back of his pants. "Anyway, he's ready to say 'I do,' but only if Aliyah will let him. Do you know if she's still up for spending the rest of her life with him?" He gave Greg a worried glance as the man stared him down.

Chrysta hesitated. She drew out an 'Uh' before things became muffled. Terrence assumed she was consulting with Aliyah before giving a reply.

"What did she say?" Greg whispered.

Terrence held up his hand to signal to wait. He tapped his foot against the floor while waiting on Chrysta.

"Aliyah's in literally no state to provide a response. I just told her Greg's ready to marry her, but she hasn't so much as budged. Give me a second to talk to her. Once I'm done, I'll call you back to let Greg know what she says. But be warned, things like these don't usually slide that easily. But for all of our sake, I hope Aliyah will be able to accept what happened and let the show go on."

Terrence agreed with that. Too much had gone down for them to just call things off. Though, he'd completely understand if Aliyah's trust in Greg had shattered. Getting cold feet on the big day was a *huge* red flag. He wasn't judging Greg, but Terrence would completely understand if Aliyah refused to marry him. The tension just got real. "Yeah. We'll stay in touch." He hung up and then rose to his feet. "Okay, Chrysta's going to talk to Aliyah, then call back, but brace yourself. Aliyah's kind of a puddle of mush."

"Thought as much." Greg groaned, then looked upward. "If she'll let me talk to her, I'll clear the air." He seemed to have many regrets.

Terrence sighed. "Let's hope for the best." He walked to the door. "Come on. We should leave. It's cramped in here."

CHAPTER NINETEEN

Chrysta held down her cell phone after conversing with Terrence. She sucked in a string of air in the doorway and then faced the inconsolable bride stretched out across the queen-sized bed in the room. Danielle had left to fetch a snack for Aliyah in the kitchen while their parents were caught up in the hall on their phones. Chrysta could bet they were speaking to guests in the yard with questions. She contemplated updating them before Aliyah but ultimately decided that her sister needed answers more urgently than they did.

Chrysta discreetly closed the door to block them from access to the room. She walked over to the dresser near Aliyah's moaning form and then leaned back against it.

What a shame. Aliyah looked so beautiful but had become nothing but a pile of sad emotions. Her makeup had run clean off with her tears, and her dress had grown wrinkled from rolling around in it. It hurt seeing such a lovely dress creased at the ends and dragging on the floor. She wished Aliyah would remove it, but Danielle's theory was that wallowing in the wedding attire was more effective for their sister. Chrysta couldn't prove this to be true but didn't dare tell Aliyah how to mourn the loss of her perfect day.

"Ally." She tapped her sister's shoulder. "Ally, come on. Greg says he's not running away anymore. He had a few doubts, but now he's ready to get married. It's up to you to say whether you're marrying him or leaving all this behind." As Chrysta poked and pinched Aliyah, she looked outside through the window beside her sister's bed. The sun had already set, and the sky had turned a rich shade of orange. The chance to marry at sunset was gone.

Aliyah continued to weep and splutter into her pillow. "I can't believe he left me at the altar!" She sounded muffled but was clear enough to understand. "Everyone knows my fiancé didn't want me." She rolled to her back and rested her limp arm on her forehead, weeping pathetically. "This is *so* humiliating!"

"Did you hear what I said?" Chrysta could guess that her sister was still in breakdown mode. "Greg is ready to say that he loves you in front of all of your guests. Do you *still* want to marry him, or has this whole 'getting cold feet' scenario left you with doubts about him?" She kicked off her heels and sat on the dresser. When her legs were hanging off the edge, her exhaustion suddenly crashed down on her like a ton of bricks. All of this back and forth just may be the death of her. She did feel for Aliyah, but her prior emptiness had returned with a vengeance. This whole ordeal reminded her of their childhood. Greg's poor actions may not have been Aliyah's fault, but staying here to comfort her sister was quite reminiscent of the times when Chrysta would clean up Aliyah's messes.

"He doesn't love me." Aliyah moped with fresh tears sprouting from her eyes. She turned them to Chrysta with a grimace. "He only feels obligated to marry me because I got knocked up. He-he… we'll probably be divorced in a matter of months. These are all signs. It's a red flag! A red flag!" She cried more with closed eyes.

Chrysta swung her legs. "So, what does this mean? Are you calling everything off? If you do, it's completely understandable. What he's done would be enough for anyone to cut a man out of their life." She'd support Aliyah no matter what she chose to do. What was essential to Chrysta now was knowing what that was.

Aliyah uncovered her forehead to stare at Chrysta. "Why would I cut him out when he's the best thing that's ever happened to me? He loves me, cares about me, looks after me, knows what he's about in life, and is an all-round perfect man. I can't leave him. And that just makes the whole thing sadder because this is the best that it gets for someone like me." She sat up abruptly. "I'm not like you, Chrys. People don't immediately see the great sides since they're all there is. I'm not perfect. Attracting someone as incredible as Greg was hard. Most men and most *people* only see me as a woman whose life isn't in order." She sniffed as she pouted and stared at her hands. "I don't have a steady job like you. I dropped out of college. Before Greg, I never had a relationship last more than a month, and with Greg, I got pregnant within the first few months of our relationship." She shook her hands and bounced where she sat as if ready to throw a level twelve tantrum. "He's the best thing I've ever had. I'm such a colossal mess!" She bawled. "I bet after you and Terrence get married, Mom and Dad will compare this fiasco to your perfect wedding by... by calling me a screw-up and a wild child like they did when we were kids. Even in adulthood, I can't get out of your shadow."

Chrysta frowned as Aliyah sobbed so hard her body seemed to convulse. "Are you being serious right now?" How did this turn into a sister war? The whole reason Chrysta had felt inadequate enough to fake her relationship with Terrence was Aliyah herself. Her and their parents' choices while raising her, of course. How dare Aliyah try to claim in any way that Chrysta had it easy? "Don't try to act like it's been a walk in the park for me, being the one who's always expected to be perfect." She hopped off the dresser with a finger aimed at her sniffling sister. "While you and Danielle have been free to make mistakes and act however you wanted, I've been tied down to the image of the perfect daughter my *entire* life!" She yelled. "My whole life, I've constantly sought validation from our parents because whenever I did anything that seemed even remotely below what they expected, they'd immediately give me crap about it. While you could slack off and get Bs and Cs if you ever felt overwhelmed at school, I had to *constantly* get good grades. God forbid I missed a lesson and did not catch up on my own time because I caught a horrible cold because if I ever did, and somehow got anything below ninety on a test, I'd never hear the end of it!"

Aliyah was suddenly dead silent.

Chrysta walked to the foot of Aliyah's bed. "And don't even get me *started* on my adulthood. Rather than taking risks at new jobs that may not necessarily fit our parents' definition of ideal, I've been *stuck* at the same corporate job doing work above my pay grade and constantly being passed over for promotion. And why is that, you ask? Oh. Because our parents believe that corporate jobs are best to boast about." She clenched her fists at her sides. "It's never been about what I want. It's always been them and what looks good for the family. I could never just exist without trying to please them. From the moment I was born, my existence was centered around *their* wants and *their* desires! Not mine! It's why I went out of my way to get a fake fiancé to call my date to your wedding. Just to not feel as if I'd let them down or as if I was behind you in life. Because you know why? It's completely unacceptable for Chrysta to be anything other than perfect!" She ended in a shout that echoed.

For the first time, Aliyah was speechless. Her puffy eyes were wide as she stared at Chrysta in nothing short of shock.

Chrysta uncurled her fists and tossed her hair off her shoulders.

Aliyah wiped her wet eyes and scooted closer to the end of her bed. "Terrence isn't actually your fiancé?"

"Of course that was all you heard." Chrysta's shoulders fell. She, too, was feeling the urge to cry but held it. All of the emotions she had held in check for so long were just bubbling out of her, but now she felt exhausted and drained. "Look, Aliyah, I'm sorry you feel that way about everything, but I've had it hard too. Being perfect all the time has taken a real toll on my mental health, and the fact that I felt the need to lie *just* to please our family shows how maddening it's been." She chuckled. "Me, a grown woman *lying* about having a fiancé. How pathetic is that? Clearly, I've lost it. This is the kind of stuff that happens in romcoms." She covered her face in embarrassment.

Surely enough, opening up to Aliyah actually helped to alleviate the weight on her shoulders. Was that what Chrysta had needed this whole time? To confess?

"I can't believe it. So, he's been acting this whole time?" Aliyah sounded more concerned with this than her own life drama.

Chrysta groaned as she dropped her hands. "Yes… I mean, no. I mean, I don't know, but we're not actually a real couple." She had memories of their time spent at his house and of the flowers he'd sent her. "Though it feels real sometimes." She stared at the ring he'd given her.

"I can't believe it." Aliyah cupped her left cheek. "But I can practically feel the chemistry when I'm around you two. He's so sweet, and you look so smitten when he's close. If it feels real, then I'm pretty sure that it's real to both of you. *Trust* me." She crossed her arms. "That's insane. If someone had told me that the way to find my one true love was to fake a relationship with them, then I would have faked a relationship with a random guy years ago."

Chrysta had to laugh. She sighed, then looked out the window. "I didn't know that was how you saw being sisters with me. This whole time, I always assumed you were making the best of not having to live up to any expectations."

Aliyah hung her legs off the foot of her bed. She swung them while rumpling the fabric of her dress in her lap. "Trust me. It's been pretty hard living in Perfect's shadow." She rubbed her shoulder. "But I should have guessed that having to be something impossible must have been hard on you too." She twisted her mouth. "Sorry for saying all of that. I would have never known you were having an awful time. It just looked so easy from the trenches where I've been. You make perfect look effortless."

"Oh, stop it." Chrysta laughed, then exhaled through her mouth. "Please don't tell anyone about the whole Terrence thing. I get the feeling it won't fly well with our folks." She could see her mother's hanging mouth now. They may just disown her on the spot if they found out. Chrysta may have been letting go of the need to please them, but she still cared what they thought of her. Just not to the extent that she'd let them rule her life.

Aliyah shook her head. "I won't need to. It's pretty obvious that you two are going to end up together." She climbed out of bed and walked to the dresser. There, she opened a small drawer and retrieved some makeup wipes. "A man doesn't just look at any woman the way Terrence looks at you. The same goes for the way you stare at him because Chrys, you seem wrapped around his finger."

Chrysta had no comment on that. Time was running out, and she could now see guests dotting the front yard as if getting ready to take off. "Look, Aliyah, you need to decide your next move. Is the wedding on or off?" She met her sister by the drawers.

Aliyah wiped off her mascara. "It's on. I just need to reapply all of this." She looked at Chrysta while cleaning her cheek. "Like I said, you don't let a man like Greg go."

This mentality was off-putting. "So, your marriage isn't about love? You just want someone who looks good beside you?" She rested her hip against the drawers.

"That's not what I mean. I mean… I love him, and he respects me, unlike the other men I've been with. I'd been so glad when he proposed, but it's probably because I'm having his child." Aliyah lowered one hand to press upon her belly.

Chrysta shook her head. "I doubt it. Terrence said that Greg only got cold feet because he was thinking of his childhood. You should know that his parents divorced and that he doesn't want that for your kid in case something happens. You talk to him all the time."

Aliyah sighed at her reflection. "I know." She seemed uneasy all of a sudden. "So, he thinks we won't last."

"Hey, hey." Chrysta held Aliyah's shoulders and turned her so that they stood face to face. "The two of you have just gone through your first major hurdle as a couple, but if you see yourself with him, and he sees himself with you, then you need to overcome it and move forward." She squeezed Aliyah gently. "Don't let the married couples on Instagram fool you into believing things need to be perfect 24-7." She could see the doubt in Aliyah's brown eyes. Mascara only remained on one, but Aliyah made this look work. "Sometimes people get scared and aren't sure what to do or what their future as a couple will look like. It doesn't mean you two are doomed. It means that you're human."

Aliyah pushed out her bottom lip and reached in for a hug.

Chrysta rubbed her sister's back with her chin against her shoulder. She thought back to the hour of the evening and the groom awaiting a response. "Okay, so should I call Terrence and let him know you're saying yes?" The hug had been broken.

Aliyah was interrupted by the creaking door. Danielle had just strut in wearing flip-flops with a new cup of tea. This one smelled like peppermint. "You'll have to give it a few blows before you drink." As her slippers clapped against the floor, she slowly changed from apathetic to curious. It was evident in how her left brow shot upward. "Did I just walk in on a heart-to-heart? Why do you guys look so sentimental?"

Chrysta stepped away as Aliyah took the tea and rested it on the dresser beside what Terrence had brought earlier. "The wedding is *back* on, Danny. Tell all the guests to sit because Greg and I are in this couple business for life." Her ecstatic party-girl persona returned as she celebrated with pumping fists.

"The wedding's back on?" Danielle bared her teeth happily. "All right! So I don't have to hunt Greg down?" She faced Chrysta with expectant eyes.

Chrysta wished she'd be less violent. "No. Because Greg was only a little unsure because of the trauma he'd experienced from watching his parents divorce as a kid." She straightened the front of her dress. "Now help Aliyah with her makeup while I try to put some order to the whole guest situation outside." She left her sisters, opening Aliyah's makeup drawer to work a miracle with little time. Things had been delayed long enough.

On her way down the carpeted stairs, Chrysta pictured Terrence. She squeezed her phone when she stepped off the last step. He and Greg needed an update. "I wonder if we *are* something real." Aliyah seemed to believe so, but the woman had never been that perceptive. "Don't get distracted." Chrysta dialed Terrence. "Yes. We're back on."

EVEN WITHOUT A DEGREE IN COSMETOLOGY, Danielle somehow managed to enhance Aliyah's natural beauty in a gentle yet bold way.

This was all Chrysta could think of while standing on the altar with the other bridesmaids. Night had fallen on what was supposed to be a sunset wedding, but they used this to their advantage. Her father and Terrence had thought quickly to combat the fading light. Together, both men intertwined some string lights into the altar's bower and plugged them into a socket. The yard's natural golden path lights complimented them well and overall gave the wedding a starlit vibe beneath the dark sky. All guests had agreed to stay to witness the late but long overdue wedding. They seemed transfixed by the impromptu lighting arrangements and had been capturing photos of the bride and groom standing within the bower.

"… and I just want to say that I'll never give you a reason to doubt me again. I'm here for you and us until death due as part." Greg was holding Aliyah's hands as he finished his vows.

Chrysta smiled at her younger sister's damp eyes. It sure had been a long day, but here they were. Aliyah began to give a tear-filled account of how they'd met and the rollercoaster they'd taken to get where they were. It must have been heart-wrenching to think one's fiancé had abandoned them, but seeing a bride completely dismantle sure had taken a toll on Chrysta, too. Had Terrence felt the same about pep-talking Greg? He'd been the first person to find him.

She found Terrence smiling among the rows of guests. *Typical Terrence,* she thought. It seemed he hadn't at all been fazed by handling Greg's tumultuous emotions. What a guy? Was anyone else as easygoing as he was?

She was floored at that moment, realizing that Terrence's easygoing nature was one of the many, many things that she loved about him.

Loved.

It filled her with hope and terror at the same time.

Aliyah's words about their chemistry and the possibility that they'd become something were suddenly all Chrysta thought about. Before they'd raced to get ready, Terrence had wanted to say something. Something Chrysta was sure she could guess on her own. The question was whether she was ready to embark on such a journey with someone she'd practically forced into her life.

Whenever she described him that way, Terrence would butt in, saying, 'I want to' or 'I chose this' or something along those lines. Chrysta supposed it was second nature for her to view herself as an inconvenience. What did she want, though? To date Terrence and possibly marry him? She liked him. He was everything she desired in a man, so why not? If he got down on one knee right now, would she say—

"Yes. I'm so happy I said yes and that we're here together. I promise to stay by your side until you breathe your last breath." Aliyah nuzzled a bashful Greg before the officiant allowed them to join lips.

Both Greg and their own parents clapped softly when the newlyweds kissed. Greg and Aliyah faced the relieved crowd, who took photos and congratulated them. Some of Greg's college buddies began a chant to which Greg beat his chest with an arm around Aliyah.

"What a beautiful ceremony," said Greg's sister to Danielle.

Chrysta overheard and had to agree. She searched for Terrence's reaction in the audience and was caught off guard after catching him staring.

The pleasant man pretended to brush sweat off his forehead while saying 'Phew' and then winked.

No other words were necessary. Chrysta caught the giggles and reacted with the same level of relief. She exaggerated hers by dropping her shoulders and staring at the heavens before holding up a thumb and mouthing, 'Thank you.'

Terrence touched his chest and bowed his head. His lips said, 'My pleasure,' and he raised his phone to capture the wonderful moment too.

Chrysta finally tuned back into the event before her. It wrapped up with Aliyah lifting her bouquet and cheering. At that point, the bridal march theme played from the stereo close by, and the bridal party began their departure from the altar.

Following her happy sister, Chrysta smiled. She was so happy for Aliyah.

But she hoped that she could keep herself from breaking down about her own fake fiancé.

CHAPTER TWENTY

Friends taking group selfies near the hedge, families uniting for talks on their futures, laughter, joy and enjoyment. Terrence surveyed the wedding, taking in all of the wonderful people celebrating the bride and groom.

It really was beautiful.

Terrence drank a gulp of his punch while standing by the wall near the seats they'd set up for the wedding. Most were empty as guests had risen to explore the property. Some caterers were currently distributing appetizers for the big reception inside the house. He'd checked up on them earlier but was back out here to observe the happy wedding attendees.

Greg and his friends were standing near the altar and grinning from ear to ear as they chatted gladly about who knew what. Terrence was just elated that Greg had moved past his insecurities. Meanwhile, Aliyah was with Chrysta and the other bridesmaids, having their pictures taken by a hired photographer. This bunch had assembled in front of the altar. He loved how beautifully each woman's dress fit their bodies.

To him, Chrysta stole the show in terms of appearances. From her makeup to how her hair curled gently past her shoulders, it was stunning. He'd had difficulty focusing on the wedding with her standing up front. The only thing his eyes would look at was her captivating face and outfit.

"Loving the punch, are we, Superman?" asked a familiar voice.

Chrysta's dad waltzed up to his side with a glass of the same beverage. "I have to admit that I am, sir," Terrence said. He held the glass up to stir its contents. "It's everything punch should be. Sweet, tasty, and refreshing."

The older man seemed to agree. "Oh yeah. We chose right with this one." He turned to look at the hedge. "Even with so many ladies dressed to impress, you're somehow still stuck on your future wife. If that isn't love, I don't know what is."

How had he noticed? Terrence scratched the back of his neck in embarrassment. "So, you've seen my eyes following her every move?"

"Yes, I have." The man nudged Terrence. "Kind of gives me hope that we won't have to worry about a possible setback when you two finally decide to have your big day." He drank from his transparent cup. "Still don't know how I feel about Greg's little stunt earlier, but I'm glad you snapped him out of it. Makes me like you even more."

Terrence couldn't blame the man for being unsure of Greg. One didn't simply recover from their daughter's groom abandoning her. Terrence was actually surprised that Aliyah had moved on so quickly. Their love seemed true, but he'd never blame her if she ever became skeptical. "I hope they'll be okay."

"Same here. They better be."

That sounded like a threat. Terrence ignored it to take in the ambiance of the backyard. He watched the small pond behind the altar. Chrysta had mentioned Aliyah's desire to have the wedding near it for nostalgia's sake. The bluish theme of the dresses was meant to represent it. More elements of the childhood the sisters had left behind were also visible in this very yard. He focused on the treehouse he'd encountered before. It wasn't hard to imagine a family living here at all. It warmed his heart that the parents never broke down the evidence of their kids' happy childhoods. Terrence hoped to one day do the same.

"Sir," he said.

"What is it, son?" The father looked him in the eye.

"Can I ask you something?"

It was almost 10 p.m., and the guests had left after a successful reception of appetizing food and fun games. Greg and Aliyah had sailed off with their 'Just Married' banner behind their vehicle and were now absent from the property. The rest of the bridal party had stayed back to assist with packing up. They'd hired help to do so. Four trucks for stacking chairs were parked out front.

Terrence stepped into the now-empty yard with hands on his hips. He whistled and walked around quietly. "Not a piece of furniture in sight."

"I know, right?" Chrysta was with him. After cleaning up inside, they'd both agreed to check for litter and any remaining debris. "You'd never believe that the biggest day of someone's life happened back here." She'd switched her heels to flats that made her significantly shorter than she had been earlier.

As they walked slowly, eyes out for anything amiss, Terrence admired the now fully visible pond. It sparkled like a diamond under the twinkling stars. He saw the moon's reflection clearly in its clear water. "I know. It's amazing how powerful props and decorations truly are. Without them, venues lose their character. Strip a place bare, and it's just a backyard again." They stopped walking at the edge of the pond.

Chrysta lowered her face as if admiring her reflection. "Not just a backyard. I mean, to kids, a backyard can be anything on the planet. A spaceship, a rodeo, heck, even a wedding scene, too." She looked at Terrence, and her face seemed to glow under all the small lights in the yard. "I vaguely remember being the minister of Ally's union with Sir Snuffs-a-Lot back when we were little. Danielle played the imaginary organ like a pro during the ceremony."

Terrence found this story endearing. "Is that so?" He put his hands in his pockets. "That makes this location even more perfect for what happened earlier. I'm touched." He noticed bright green fireflies over the hedge between this property and the neighbor's. He heard noises from inside Chrysta's old house that told him they'd finished up the cleaning. Someone had just turned on some eighties classics that blared from the stereo. There was talking and chuckles happening in there, too. It filled him with a fuzzy warmth.

"I must have already explained why Ally wanted her wedding here. She wanted to fulfill the wishes of her inner child." Chrysta took a deep breath. "And though things didn't go exactly according to plan, they were close enough to how she'd imagined it." She smiled at him.

Terrence could see the fireflies multiplying. They were buzzing their way toward them. "And what about you? Did you ever get married to a stuffed animal out here?" He attempted a joke, which worked. Chrysta's laugh was everything.

"Aliyah was the one itching for a perfect wedding. Though I *do* remember kissing a 'pretend-frog' out here to turn him back into a prince." She covered her face with one hand. "It's amazing how kids will re-enact whatever they read or see on TV." Chrysta sighed almost wistfully, then walked him away from the pond. "Do you see that treehouse?"

Terrence envisioned children climbing up the rope ladder to play tag within the small wooden structure. "It's adorable. Too bad it needs some repairs done." He gestured a hand in front of it. "If I had the time, I'd come by here on a weekend and make some adjustments myself. Maybe Aliyah's kid can find new ways to play around it. Times have changed, but all kids like treehouses, right?"

"Mhmm!" Chrysta opened her palm toward the tree. "I was just about to say something similar." She pointed to the missing door. "I'd break that down and create a doorway that seems a little more magical and work on expanding what's already there. As kids, we'd have tea parties up there, but there wasn't much running room. I want running room for my kids."

"Oh, so your kids will be playing in the treehouse too?" Terrence's heart did a flip.

"Well..." Chrysta stroked her hair. "That's the dream." She shrugged. "I'd been extremely caught up with impressing my parents before, but this whole wedding experience has allowed me some time to think about what *I* want and what that means for me." Somehow, her aura grew in radiance. Fireflies continued to dot the scene as small green lights.

Terrence wished he'd brought a camera to snap a candid shot of her. Chrysta's beauty at this instant could not be easily described. He needed evidence that he'd witnessed it. "That's great." He loved that for her. "And..." He moved closer. "What do you want aside from tons of kids? A big house? A new job? Someone to share your life with?"

She seemed to notice he'd closed in. "And what if I said yes to everything you listed?" Chrysta's voice had softened just now. "Hey."

"Hey."

"Before we'd all begun to get ready, you'd wanted to tell me something."

Terrence looked down as she faced him. If he leaned in any closer, their noses might touch. "Wow, you remember."

She nodded. "If you'd wanted to say something along the lines of 'We should try being something for real,' then I just want to let you know that I do see it. And... I want it. We may not have gotten to know each other traditionally, but somehow that makes us more special." Chrysta reached for his hand, and Terrence saw fireworks. "I like you a lot, Terrence. And apparently, everyone's been able to see that we can work but me."

This was all music to Terrence's ears. "What can I say to that?" he whispered while smiling in satisfaction. "I guess it'd only make sense to let you know that I fell in love with you right off the bat."

Chrysta blinked delicately. "Really?"

"No exaggeration." And now he was thinking of what he'd asked her dad. "We started getting to know each other for the whole fake fiancé charade, and the more I spent time with you, the more I wanted to be close. To have you as my own and share a life with you." His chest tightened as Chrysta's eyes sparkled with intrigue. "It was just hard to say all of that, considering our situation. But since you let me know that you want us to be, then I can finally tell you." He took her other hand and was overcome with happiness when she held him back tightly. "I *do* love you. So much that it's insane. At night, I daydream about what we'd be in the future and what my life might look like if you became my wife." He stared at the intertwined fingers between their bodies. Chrysta held him as tightly as he held her. "It sounds crazy, but my dad always said a man knew when he knew, and for me, I know it's you." He met her infatuated eyes. "Tell me to stop if I'm saying too much."

"You haven't said enough." Chrysta's voice shivered with something that sounded like anticipation. She was excited to hear him speak.

And he wanted to tell her more.

Her spoken words gave Terrence the okay. "Do you mean it? Because I talked to your dad, and if you'd like me to use the permission he granted me, I will." He got so close that he swore he heard her heart racing like a sports car.

"At this point, it feels like we already are what we've fooled everyone into believing, so go ahead." Chrysta bit her lower lip as if both nervous and excited.

Terrence's smile was gradual and wide enough that his cheeks ached at the effort. "Will you marry me?"

Chrysta's reaction reminded him of a sunset, mellow but with all the fire and dedication that he loved about Chrysta. She fixed him with a stare, and then a slow smile spread across her lips. Holding his gaze for just one more minute, she paused.

Then, she said the word that changed Terrence's world forever. "Yes."

D *ing*
"There they are." Terrence waved to Aliyah and Greg before Chrysta could scan the crowded diner. He motioned for them to come over, and they pressed their way through the throng of people.

"Chryssie and Terrence! So good to see you two," Aliyah chirped. With Greg's help, Aliyah rose from the small booth she'd been sitting in. Just standing looked like a chore for her. She quickly touched her enlarged stomach and caught her breath beside the table. "Dang it," she muttered, looking down at her stomach. "You're getting in the way here, baby."

"Don't strain yourself. We're coming." Chrysta squeezed Terrence's hand tightly as they walked past full tables of conversing patrons. The diner had never looked more alive. With the Fall Harvest Festival taking place this afternoon on Main Street, Chrysta wasn't surprised. Heading there alone had become customary for her every year, but now that she had the sweetest man to call her fiancé, that simply wouldn't do. He'd driven all the way from Peachwood to ensure she had a date. They tended to alternate. It'd been months since they'd agreed to be together but hadn't moved in with each other yet. The hunt for an apartment was still on, but for now, commuting for dates was how they operated. They'd both agreed to work out the technicalities of who'd move where based on which town offered better apartments.

Aliyah wrapped her arms around Chrysta when they met by her table while Terrence and Greg shared a fist-bump. Both couples found themselves seated after.

Chrysta breathed in the aromatic scent of pastries and sausages after settling in beside the window. She still attended book club meetings weekly but wasn't a regular customer here. The only seat she was accustomed to was where they'd hold meetings. Sitting here was odd. She twisted herself to get an idea of her surroundings and noticed Rochelle sitting in the spot behind them with Mrs. Zhang. A brief flashback of how this all started played through her head like a movie. Were they gossiping again? If so, would overhearing them lead Chrysta to another incredibly life-changing experience?

"Why are you smiling? Are you that excited for the festival later?" Aliyah's hair had grown fuller, and her face was as clear as a child's. It seemed pregnancy was treating her well. The beige sweater covering her top half brought out the warmth in her eyes.

"No. I was just remembering something." Chrysta spotted a waiter coming their way. When they each ordered what they wanted, she heaved a sigh of contentment. "So soon, little Tommy will be running around Sweetgum, huh?"

Terrence laughed with his arm around her shoulders. "How many times do they have to say his name isn't Tommy?" His other arm was on the table. The diner had a fall menu and orange-leaf decorations hanging from the ceiling. They'd put on the heat to combat the chilling weather. Chrysta could see the wind tossing up real leaves littering the sidewalk.

"He's her nephew. I say Chrysta can experiment with names all she wants. Who knows? Aliyah and I just might consider one of them." Greg's forest green turtleneck was of the finest fabrics. He rubbed his hands against the mug they'd met him holding. "The pregnancy's coming along fine, so if all goes well, the family will see its first Greg Junior."

Chrysta rolled her eyes at the corny name. "Anything but Greg Junior. Junior names are so uncreative."

"They also show a level of vanity, in my opinion, but that's just me." Terrence turned to look out the window. "I think that once you finally get to hold him in your arms and stare into his precious face for the first time, you'll know exactly what to name him." He pretended to hold a baby by motioning his arms as if rocking one. "I've heard a lot of moms describe what it's like seeing their child for the first time, and they make it seem as if everything clicks. Like life finally has a purpose now that they've brought someone else into the world." He scratched his head. "But I'm just guessing. I'll never know what it's like to give birth."

"You described it like you do." That was what Chrysta loved about him. Terrence had to be the most empathetic man alive. People's feelings were important to him, and it showed. He seemed capable of putting himself in anyone's shoes. More dates and late-night conversations had taught this to her well. "But thanks for acknowledging that you won't quite get what childbirth is like. I mean, it's beautiful, but we all know before the beauty, there needs to be the ugly." Chrysta winced as Aliyah rolled her eyes. Greg hid his laugh poorly.

"Yes, yes. I know. The hundreds of childbirth videos and accounts from mothers taught me everything. Do you know that you bombard people with information?" Aliyah folded her arms over her large belly. She stopped to massage it.

Chrysta gasped. "What? It's just my way of helping." She pinched Terrence, who started to laugh. Ever since her heart-to-heart with Aliyah before the wedding, they'd been much closer. Before, she'd hesitated to call Aliyah a companion, but now, they were practically best friends. And all it took was one heartfelt conversation. Their improved relationship was proof that communication was key to building anything long-lasting with someone. If only she'd thought of that sooner.

When their food was brought before them, Aliyah devoured her two pie slices with zeal. Greg had begun to break down her cravings and what they usually meant until his cell phone rang. It seemed the call was important because he'd gotten up to answer it near the exit. Aliyah took the opportunity to eat in silence while Terrence insisted she slow down.

Chrysta laughed at her sister's insatiable appetite before catching Rochelle walking past them to settle in the seat Chrysta had seen her in prior. When had the older woman risen? In fact, why wasn't she behind the diner at a time like this? There were so many customers coming in and out. From here, it looked like the front desk employees were overworked. Was Rochelle perhaps on break?

Rather than interrupting the woman's lunch date with questions, Chrysta instead opted to eavesdrop just like she'd done a few months ago. Who knew? Maybe doing so would bring good fortune, just like last time.

"… from my knees to my ankles. Oh, you have no idea how hard it's been on these old bones running this diner. I love it to death, but the body's showing signs it needs rest," Rochelle complained.

"Humph." Mrs. Zhang seemed to be chewing. Chrysta refused to turn around in case she was caught. "I completely understand. I was reading this article online that said if older folk don't retire, they'll end up stuck on the grind till the very day they die. Now, for some, that's heaven, but for others, it's hell. Absolute hell." She huffed again. "They say it's great to keep working so the mind stays active, but if it's wearing you down, then I think you have a right to kick back. What do you say?"

Rochelle grumbled some words. "Yes, yes, I know. I'm planning on retiring soon, but for now, I just want to enjoy my last moments running the old place."

"This place will feel really strange without you in charge," said Mrs. Zhang. "But you know what they say: out with the old and in with the new. Who's the young whipper-snapper you've chosen to take over?"

Rochelle began to explain how she was still in the process of choosing.

Chrysta was rather satisfied with the answer she'd gotten but somehow could not pull her ears away from their discussion. It seemed Terrence had gotten engrossed in their talking, too. He no longer spoke with Aliyah but instead sat in silence with occasional eyes shooting at their backs. She supposed that meant they had more in common than she'd initially anticipated. Had he deduced that she'd tuned into the women's conversation? Why would Terrence be remotely interested in anything two old women had to say?

Rochelle seemed to make up her mind. "So, it's just down to two candidates for now, but I'm taking my time."

"Great. It's always nice seeing youngsters take an interest in running businesses." Mrs. Zhang seemed delighted by what she'd been informed. "It's just like my son, Alex. You know, he'll be moving back into town soon. He has his own business, and it has been thriving. He's like those handsome CEOs in the romance novels." She laughed. "The boy is just always busy with work but somehow can't take his mind off the God-awful ex he left recently."

"Oh, that girl?" Rochelle made a noise of revulsion. "Never met her, but I trust when you say she was the devil incarnate. I hope he finds someone better here in Sweetgum. Our town is just swimming with beautiful women. There must be one for him."

"You made them sound like fish in the sea. Oh, wait, that's the saying!"

Mrs. Zhang and Rochelle cackled together for absurdly long.

Terrence snorted, and Chrysta knew exactly why he'd done so. "So, you really are listening," she whispered slyly to the man.

"Listening to what?" Aliyah wiped her mouth and stood up slowly.

"Hey, hey, where are you going?" Terrence almost got up, too, when she started limping away from their table. Greg was still on the phone.

Aliyah fanned him away like a pest. "Relax. I just need to use the bathroom. It comes with the pregnancy." She held her belly and left them alone.

Chrysta watched closely as her sister left the scene and then nudged Terrence with her elbow. "I saw you laugh just now at how those two women laughed." She spoke directly into his ear. "You've been eavesdropping on their conversation." She wagged a finger after pulling away. "Shame on you, Terrence. Shame. On. You."

"Shame on me?" He held his chest in evident fake surprise. "You only know I was listening in because you were. I saw you reacting to everything they said and put two and two together." He pressed his lips to her cheek when he spoke.

The stroke of his breath tickled her skin. "I actually know them, so it's less weird on me," Chrysta said smugly. She cocked her head sideways. "What were they saying that was so engrossing to you anyway? They couldn't have possibly been discussing football or any of the other things you like."

Terrence poked her chest. "You tell me."

"No, I want to know what you deduced while paying attention for so long." She rubbed her nose against his face.

Terrence shook his head before holding her hand under the table. "Oh, you know. They were just looking our way and saying how much of a cute couple we are." He kissed her hand, and she rested against him after erupting in smitten giggles.

AUTHOR'S NOTE

Thank you so much for reading Secret Sweethearts, the seventh book in the Sweetgum Meadows Romance series of stand-alone novels. I really hope you loved it! If you enjoyed this book, please consider leaving it a review so that others may also find it. Also, if you haven't read the first book in the series yet, check it out today!

I look forward to introducing you to the other characters in this lovely, family-oriented town where each couple will find their happily ever after. So join me with book 8, Endless Love, to meet Mrs. Zhang's son, Alex, and watch him find his happily ever after.

Would you like to receive bonus scenes and keep up with what's next with my upcoming books? Then, make sure you sign up for my mailing list on my website by visiting ImaniPrice.com.

ALSO BY IMANI PRICE

Book 1: Love Between Us

Book 2: Sweet Sunsets

Book 3: Infinite Kiss

Book 4: Dance With Me

Book 5: In Charge

Book 6: Forever With You

Book 7: Secret Sweethearts

Book 8: Endless Love

Book 9: The Harder We Fall

Book 10: Reservations of the Heart

Book 11: Play by Play

Book 12: Guarded Hearts

Book 13: Healing Hearts

Book 14: Dear Sweetgum

Book 15: Lanterns of the Meadows (novella)

Book 16: Drawn to You

Book 17: Under the Sweetgum Tree

Sweetgum Meadows' Visitor's Guide

My full audiobook catalog is available for FREE on YouTube. Check it out here: https://swiy.co/Sweetgum

To all my lovely readers,

Thank you for reading

www.ingramcontent.com/pod-product-compliance
Lightning Source LLC
Chambersburg PA
CBHW061350310726
48974CB00001B/281